PICKLED WATERMELON

ESTY SCHACHTER

KAR-BEN
PUBLISHING

KAR-BEN PUBLISHING
A division of Lerner Publishing Group, Inc.
241 First Avenue North
Minneapolis, MN 55401 USA
1-800-4-KARBEN

Website address: www.karben.com

Cover illustration by Alex Orbe.

Main body text set in Bembo Std Regular 12.5/17.
Typeface provided by Monotype Typography.

Library of Congress Cataloging-in-Publication Data

Names: Schachter, Esty, author.
Title: Pickled watermelon / by Esty Schachter.
Description: Minneapolis : Kar-Ben Publishing, [2018] | Series: Israel |
    Summary: In the summer of 1986, Molly visits her grandparents in
    mysterious Israel and worries about the language barrier.
Identifiers: LCCN 2017031306| ISBN 9781541542334 (th) |
    ISBN 9781512499902 (pb) | ISBN 9781512499919 (eb pdf)
Subjects: | CYAC: Israel—Social life and customs—20th century—Fiction. |
    Family life—Israel—Fiction. | Jews—Israel—Fiction. | Grandparents—
    Fiction. | Language and languages—Fiction.
Classification: LCC PZ7.S3288 Pi 2018 | DDC [Fic]—dc23

LC record available at https://lccn.loc.gov/2017031306

Manufactured in the United States of America
2-1009180-33371-1/11/2023

FOR MY GRANDPARENTS. THIS MAY BE A WORK
OF FICTION, BUT ALL THE LOVE IN IT IS REAL

1

"That's not a word, Bubbe."

"It is a word. Look it up," my grandmother said, scowling the way she always does when I catch her trying to get away with something.

"That's Yiddish, Bubbe. You know the rules: no names, no places, no Yiddish."

Bubbe couldn't stop herself from smiling. "Who says you always have to follow the rules?" she teased. "Anyway, enough already. You win. And your mother will be here soon."

"We're tied." I rolled the wooden letters off the board and into the Scrabble box and then pushed the pieces around with my finger. "I guess we'll play our next match when I get back."

"Of course. Why wouldn't we?"

I knew my grandmother was looking at me,

waiting for me to answer, but I stared at the tiles instead.

"For such a big trip, Molly, you don't seem so excited." Bubbe put the cover on the box and stood up. She walked into the kitchen and brought back a plate of cookies, the *rogelach* we'd baked the day before. The apartment still smelled of cinnamon and melted butter. She handed one to me.

"Tell me, what's the big problem? You'll visit Israel for one month, spend time with the family, go to the wedding, and then you'll be back so soon."

It sounded simple when Bubbe said it, but to me, it was impossible to imagine. A whole month in a foreign country with people I didn't know, people who spoke a different language. This wasn't how I'd expected to spend the summer of 1986. Not at all.

I bit small pieces of cookie, making the dough chip off in layers in my mouth. "It's not a *problem*, really," I answered, wishing I could tell Bubbe how I felt. But I wasn't saying anything to anyone, especially not my parents. I knew they'd just think I was being melodramatic. But I was used to spending summer at camp with my friends, especially my best friend Jenny.

"Well, I know that if *I* was going to fly far away and meet people I had never seen before, I might be a little nervous," Bubbe said as she swept up cookie crumbs with her palm. "But you'll enjoy yourself once you get there. Your grandparents have waited a long time to meet you and your brother. All the other relatives too. I can't imagine what it would be like not to know you. It will be exciting for all of you."

"But Bubbe, they don't speak any English."

At Hebrew school I'd only learned to recite a few words of Hebrew. I remembered a few basics like mother and father—*ima* and *abba*; food—*ochel*; and bathroom—*beit shimush*. My class had certainly heard *sheket bevakasha*—quiet, please!—often enough. But that vocabulary wasn't going to get me far if I wanted to talk to my relatives.

Back when we were really little, my mother taught Ben and me to call our grandparents *Savta* and *Saba*, Hebrew for "grandmother" and "grandfather." I spoke on the phone to my grandparents a couple of times a year, reciting lines my mother taught me: "*Yom Huledet Sameach*, Savta," on Savta's birthday, "*Shana Tova*, Saba," on Rosh Hashanah, the Jewish New Year. They would respond somehow, and then

Mom would take back the phone. I couldn't imagine spending a whole month like that.

"*I* didn't always speak English, you know," Bubbe told me now. "It will be okay. You will get to know them and then you will come back here and describe everyone in such detail that I will feel like I have been there myself." Bubbe smiled, and I tried to smile back. It's hard not to smile back at Bubbe.

"Mom's told us a little about them, and I've seen pictures . . ." But in my mind, all those relatives were just that, photographs, flat and unfamiliar.

"I met your grandparents once, years ago, when I went to Israel for your parents' wedding. Your grandmother knew how to make me laugh. Your grandfather was shy, like you."

"Are they anything like you?" I asked.

"In some ways, maybe. We come from the same beginning, all the way back to Romania, but with different countries and so many years we are probably very, very different. Anyway, what do you need with more than one of me?" Bubbe laughed and put her hand on my cheek, and I leaned my head into her palm.

The doorbell rang. Bubbe put her hand on my shoulder and squeezed it. "I know you love writing in your journal and making up stories. Think of this as a chance to find new stories for yourself. Try to enjoy it."

The doorbell rang again, more insistently this time. I suddenly wished I could press a magic button that would let me stay with this grandmother, in my own town, with my own friends, for as long as I wanted.

No such luck. "Okay, okay, we're coming!" Bubbe shouted. She went to the door and let my mother in.

My mother walked into the apartment out of breath, holding a suitcase I didn't recognize. "What a crazy day! We couldn't find Ben's suitcase, so I had to go out and get another one. Then Dad looked at the plane tickets and realized we weren't all sitting together. It took an hour to get that changed . . ."

Mom had been wrapped up in planning this trip for ages. It had been three years since she last visited her family. She and Dad had carefully planned and saved so that all four of us could go to Israel for my uncle's wedding. It had taken weeks to pack. Mom chose small gifts for each relative, worrying about who would like what the most. Ben and I listened to long lists of funny-sounding names belonging to people who were apparently my cousins, aunts, and uncles. I knew I wouldn't be able to remember them—the names all sounded so different from our own. And through it all, I couldn't shake one major question:

Who are these people?

Is it possible to think of people you have never, ever met as your family? And how in the world was I supposed to get to know them when we couldn't speak each other's languages?

Mom sighed and grabbed a cookie. "I can't wait until we're there already."

I really wished I felt the same way.

Dear Bubbe,

    While I'm gone, I've decided to write my journal entries as if they're letters to you. That way you won't feel so far away—and you can read them when I get home. I'm writing this from the airplane on the way to Israel.

    In case you were wondering, twelve hours on a plane is a long time.

    Twelve hours is two school days back to back. Three trips in the car from New York to Boston. Forty-eight bike rides from my house to yours, in a row.

    Ben and I have already played at least fifteen games of Uno. Even watching movies gets old when you've done it for so long. So I'm actually relieved that the pilot just announced that the plane is about to land. I'll write more when we get to Nahariya, the town where Savta and Saba live.

● ● ●

My mother was beginning to act strangely.

While we waited for the plane to finish its descent, Mom picked up her purse, put on some lipstick, and checked her face in the mirror. Then, about a minute later, she wiped off the lipstick with a tissue and repeated the routine with a new color. When she started on a third round, my father interrupted her and held her hand. The whole thing was weird. I tried to ignore them both by looking out the plane window.

I felt my ears pop as the plane began to land. When the plane's wheels bounced lightly on the ground, I allowed myself to make a wish. It was something I thought about all the time lately but would never tell anyone else. I wished that I would like my grandparents, and that they would like me.

The plane coasted down the runway for a few minutes and came to a stop. Music came on in the cabin, and the passengers clapped loudly. My mother explained that the applause was for the good trip and safe landing. Ben and I looked at each other and raised our eyebrows. Having an eight-year-old brother is a pain 90 percent of the time, but once in a while, Ben is okay.

We climbed down a long set of stairs into the hot summer air. Flight attendants waved us onto a bus that drove us to the main terminal. There we waited in a long line to have our passports checked. My head felt heavy and achy. Being awake most of the night on a plane will do that to you. The noise from so many people crammed together didn't help.

Once we were through the line, we went to find our luggage. Dozens of people crowded around the enormous conveyor belt. All around me people talked loudly, and I couldn't understand any of it. Once we'd gathered our belongings, we continued through customs and then headed to a doorway leading outside.

I was in no way prepared to see the massive crowd waiting on the other side of that door. People stood behind a metal gate, calling out to the emerging passengers. My mother searched the faces. I held onto my suitcase so tightly that my knuckles turned white. Suddenly my mother yelled something and rushed forward past the other passengers, around the gate, and into the crowd. My father followed, pulling me and Ben with him.

Suddenly an old woman was hugging me tightly. When she let go, another woman held my face in her hands, and an old man kissed my forehead. A younger man ruffled my hair. The old woman was crying, and when I looked up, I saw that my mother was crying too.

There was more kissing, more hugging, and then we were all ushered into a cab that looked like a stretched-out car with three rows of seats. I'd never seen anything like it at home. It was hot inside, even with all the windows rolled down. As the cab pulled away from the airport, I looked at the people around me. Growing up, I'd seen them in photographs, but for the first time they were right in front of me. My grandmother was short and plump, with long gray hair tied into a bun. My grandfather was thin and wore suspenders and wire-rimmed glasses. Aunt Rivka, Mom's sister, had long, brown, curly hair and didn't wear any makeup. Uncle Meir had bright blue eyes and very short dark hair. Meir was my mother's baby brother, the one she always bragged about. It was his wedding we'd come all this way to celebrate.

I leaned my head against the window, listening to Mom speak in Hebrew to her parents and siblings. Their voices grew quieter and quieter. My eyes couldn't stay open.

I woke up to my father gently saying my name. The van was parked in front of a house that looked like a large white box with a flat roof. My mother and grandfather seemed to be arguing over who would carry the luggage, as Dad carried Ben, still asleep, out of the cab. I followed them past a garden and up several stairs into the small house. My father explained that my grandparents lived on the first floor and another family lived on the second. Once everything was set down and Ben put to bed in one of the other rooms, the rest of us all gathered around the kitchen table. My grandmother put a plate of chocolate wafers on the table, looked at me, and turned to my mother, speaking to her in Hebrew.

"Savta wants to know if you would like some milk."

"Sure," I answered, not knowing whether to look at my mother or my grandmother.

Savta took a container out of the refrigerator, poured milk into a cup, and silently placed the cup in front of me. Each time one of my relatives looked at me, I couldn't help but smile nervously. That's what I do when I don't quite know what else to do.

Aunt Rivka showed us photographs of her children. "Molly, Molly, you are so sweet," she repeated over and over. When she laughed she sounded just like my mother.

Even though I really was trying very hard to stay awake, my eyes began to close again. My uncle noticed and laughed. I felt myself blush and wished everyone would stop looking at me.

"Of course you're tired," he said softly, like he knew what I was thinking. "There's a seven-hour time difference, so even though it's the afternoon here, you've been up all night!"

Moments later I found myself tucked into a cot just like Ben's. My father shut the door, and in the dark, I could feel my heart pounding. It was too much! Too many people and things I didn't understand and didn't know. I took a deep breath.

How would I make it through a month of this?

3

I opened my eyes the next morning and had no idea where I was.

My head hurt a little, and my legs were sore too. As I looked around the room, the journey to my new grandparents—new to me, anyway—all came back. I'd followed the pilot's advice and changed my watch to local time, and that's how I knew it was only five thirty in the morning. Still, I was wide awake. I heard the sound of the sea outside, but when I looked out the window all I saw was the white wall of a neighbor's house behind a row of overgrown bushes.

I crawled out of bed and wandered into the kitchen.

"Molly, come in! Good morning, you are the first awake. Come sit." Aunt Rivka pointed to a chair.

I smiled nervously at her and sat down at the kitchen table—which was covered with rolls, tomatoes, cucumbers, hunks of cheese, and several plastic containers. Savta stood at the sink, washing dishes. She turned to Rivka and said a few words in Hebrew.

"Savta says good morning and wants to know if you slept well?"

"Yes, thank you. Good morning."

"Would you like some breakfast?" Rivka asked, speaking quickly as she pointed to different containers. "Here is some *leben*, which is like yogurt; here's cottage cheese; this one is the butter. Be careful with the vegetable knife; it's very sharp. Meir had to leave late last night for Tel Aviv, but he asked me to tell you that he was sorry he didn't have a chance to talk more with you. I'm leaving in a minute—I have to get back for work! I'm going back to the *kibbutz* today, but I will see you later this week."

Rivka stood up, wiping her mouth with a napkin. She waved to Savta, who waved back with a soapy hand. Before I could react, she had kissed me on the top of my head and rushed out of the kitchen. A moment later I heard the screen door close behind her.

Savta dried her hands on a thin towel that looked like an old piece of cloth. We smiled at each other for an awkwardly long moment before Savta pointed her finger at the food and then at me, mumbling some words I couldn't understand. I always eat cereal for breakfast and didn't quite know what to do with what was in front of me. I shrugged my shoulders, hoping my grandmother would somehow understand and let me wait for my parents. Instead, Savta picked up a tomato and chopped it into small cubes, then dumped them into a bowl and poured yogurt over them. She thumped me on the back and went back to the sink. I stared at this breakfast, totally confused. I moved the pieces of tomato around with a spoon, sniffed the mixture, then touched the tip of my tongue to the tip of the spoon.

"Trying something new?" Dad asked as he walked into the kitchen. He smiled and winked. "It took me a long time to get used to salad for breakfast. Give it a try, and if you don't like it, we'll go out later and hunt down a box of cornflakes."

I thought his offer sounded reasonable, so I tasted the new concoction. The mixture didn't taste sweet, the way I'd expected, but tangy and cool in my mouth. I ate a few more spoonfuls before giving up. My father looked up from the cucumber he was slicing.

"Cornflakes," I whispered.

"Fair enough." He started buttering a roll. "It'll take a few days, but then we'll all adjust to the time change and stop waking up so early."

"Does *she* always wake up so early?" I nodded toward my grandmother.

"Always. Your grandfather is already at the store. He's up at dawn and goes out to get the fish and chickens he'll sell for the day. Savta will go down in a little while to help him."

"Is it like a supermarket?"

"No, not at all. He buys the fish live and—well, you'll see when we go visit."

"Are the chickens alive too?"

"Not anymore. But your grandparents used to have a coop out behind the house. Now your grandfather buys them from someone."

Savta worked busily at the counter, mixing ingredients in a large pot. She spoke on and off to Dad, who answered slowly and in what seemed to be very short sentences.

"Dad, you talk really slowly when you speak Hebrew," I said.

He laughed. "Well, I wouldn't exactly say I *speak* Hebrew. I might say I destroy the language. I haven't spoken regularly in fifteen years, and even back then I fumbled a lot."

"Mom speaks Hebrew to you at home sometimes."

"Sometimes."

Mom talked to Dad in Hebrew whenever she had something to tell him that she didn't want me or Ben to understand. Their secret language had always annoyed me. Could I actually learn enough during this trip to understand what they were saying?

"How long did you live here?" I asked, looking for some sense of what I could expect to learn in a month.

"Eight months at a stretch. After that I visited your mother twice, but only for a few weeks at a time."

My enthusiasm faded as quickly as it had bloomed. I resigned myself to stumbling along and trying to pick up as many Hebrew words as possible before it was time to leave.

A few minutes later, Mom and Ben joined us. Ben, cranky as ever, wouldn't even try the yogurt mixture, especially not after I taunted him with some of mine. I chewed on a piece of bread and salty butter, watching my mother and grandmother chat.

After a while I left the kitchen to explore the rest of the house. I discovered that the bathroom was actually two small rooms: one with the toilet and another with a sink, a bathtub, and a simple shower—just a showerhead and a drain in the floor. Even the bathrooms were different here!

I peeked into my parents' room, which looked similar to the one I shared with Ben. A sofa bed, chairs, and a table filled the space. Shelves on the wall held wooden figurines, photographs, and circles of lace. A side door led to a little terrace.

My grandparents' room was next door. On one side of the room, wedged between the wall and the huge bed, stood a large bureau with a mirror on the top. I looked at my reflection in the mirror and saw a girl with long, curly, brown hair and a smudge of yogurt on her chin. I wiped the yogurt off and noticed something else in the mirror's reflection: a big framed photograph on the wall behind me. I turned around and studied it, counting nine people—two pairs of adults and five children. I recognized younger versions of Savta and Saba, so I knew one of these children must be my mother, even though I couldn't pick out which one. No one smiled in the picture. Everyone looked straight ahead, serious—and, I thought, sad. I couldn't help wondering why.

My eyes drifted to a smaller photo on a shelf. This image was just as crowded, but the people in it wore more old-fashioned clothing. Looking from one photograph to the other, I guessed that one of the young men in the older picture was Saba. So these others must be his parents and siblings . . . I tried to remember the names Mom and Dad had mentioned over the years, but the only one that came to me was Malka, the great-aunt I'd been named for. She was Saba's sister, so she was probably one of the girls in this picture. I scanned each face, as if I might recognize her somehow. Some of the girls looked a little like me. It was strange to think that different versions of my face had been floating around Europe, and then Israel, long before I was born.

Finally, I went back to my own room and sat on my cot, listening to the muffled sounds of my family speaking to each other as they ate. Could I really be the only one feeling confused and more than a little bit lost?

Ben marched into the room. "Mom and Dad say to get dressed and we'll go visit Saba at the store." He opened his suitcase and began digging through his clothes. "Mom said it's going to be hot today, at least ninety degrees."

"Where are you getting dressed?" I asked, tapping my foot on the stone floor.

"Right here, what'd you think?"

"Then where am *I* supposed to change?"

Ben shrugged his shoulders. "How should I know?"

"Mom!"

I ended up waiting outside while Ben dressed. I knew I could have just as easily gone into the bathroom, but I didn't feel like backing down. *This is ridiculous,* I thought angrily. *I'm eleven—way too old to be sharing a room with an eight-year-old boy! I want to go home.*

I leaned against the door, closed my eyes, breathed in, breathed out, and waited.

4

Savta waved to us from the window as we walked down the path through the garden. Two blocks away from my grandparents' house, we came to a large square, which was already busy at eight in the morning. Stores lined two sides of it, and on the third stood a bus stop. A crowd of people dressed in bathing suits and holding towels was gathered there. In the center of the square, elderly people sat on benches, talking to one another.

My mother led us into one of the small shops. Saba came out from behind a long wooden counter to hug us. He wore baggy pants and suspenders and a gray felt hat. Thin, muscular arms stuck out from his loose white shirtsleeves. Behind him, a tiled tub stood attached to the wall. The tub came up to Saba's waist. Ben ran over to it and peered in.

"Molly, come look. Fish!"

At least fifteen enormous fish swam around each other in the tub. I had never seen fish so big and so alive—usually they were lying flat on ice in a supermarket case.

"They're carp, Ben. Bubbe makes her gefilte fish out of them," Dad explained.

I couldn't quite imagine how the thin slices of sweet gefilte fish that I loved so much came from the ugly, gray carp swimming in the tank. Their eyes looked like yellow marbles flattened into either side of their heads.

A woman with a scarf wrapped around her head walked into the store. Saba introduced my parents to her. He pointed to Ben and me and beamed. The woman put her hands up to her face and shook her head back and forth, talking in a high-pitched voice. I looked to my father and raised my eyebrows.

"She's an old customer of your grandfather's and can't believe we're here all the way from America. She says she remembers coming to the store on the day you were born, Molly."

I smiled at the woman, who continued crooning over us. Saba motioned toward the tank, and the woman raised one finger. Saba picked up a large net with a long wooden handle and leaned over the tank. Suddenly he brought the net down into the water and scooped out a flapping fish. The fish beat against the mesh, spraying water on the floor. Saba dumped the fish on the table and held it down with one hand. Then he took a wooden club and hit the fish quick and hard on its head. He wrapped the fish in newspaper, and I saw a few spots of blood appear on the newsprint. Saba handed the fish to the woman and took her payment. She was still chattering as she walked out the door.

I turned away and looked at Ben, who was staring at the fish swimming in the tank.

"Do you think it hurts them?" he whispered.

"I don't know."

"Do you think they know what's going to happen to them?"

"Of course not." At least I hoped not.

After a few minutes, we left the store and walked around the square. We passed a butcher, a tailor, the post office, a vegetable market, a shoemaker, and a store filled with cookies and candy. Mom said there was a toy store in the back of the candy shop. Each business owner greeted my mother warmly, with a shout and a hug. At the butcher shop, Ben and I waited outside, afraid of what we might see if we went in. A burly man with gray hair came out to see us and pinch our cheeks. The candy store was my favorite, especially since the elderly couple behind the counter immediately began filling a bag with a whole assortment of sweets for us. I also got a glass bottle of Coke. I had never drunk Coke from a bottle, and I loved the Hebrew writing on the side. I decided to save it for Bubbe to see.

Walking home, we passed Savta on her way to the store. She spoke briefly to my mother before she continued on her way. Back at the house, Ben and I sifted through our strange new candy. Ben found several pieces of Bazooka bubble gum, with the wrapper printed in Hebrew. We bit into a few delicious chocolate wafers and candy bars until Dad made us promise not to eat any more before lunch. We played checkers on the cool stone path—and couldn't help squealing as tiny green lizards darted around us.

At noon, Saba and Savta came back from the store and we all sat down to lunch. Lunch looked like what I usually call dinner—salad followed by chicken and potatoes. Savta passed around a plate of pickles to go with the meat. There were regular pickles—the kind made out of cucumbers—plus small, green pickled tomatoes and chunks of something pink and green.

"What is that?" Ben asked when he spotted the chunks.

"That's pickled watermelon, a Romanian specialty your grandmother makes." Mom took a piece and popped it into her mouth. "Try it. It's salty, not sweet."

"No, thanks, it looks weird," Ben said, wrinkling his nose.

"You're making a big mistake. This is great stuff." Dad took several pieces and put them on his plate. "I'm stocking up before you realize how good it is. I want to make sure there's enough for me."

I pierced a chunk with my fork and held it up in front of my face. It smelled like the other pickles. I tasted it. The white rind was soft and chewy, and the salty, garlicky watermelon flesh tasted delicious. This was certainly my best discovery yet. I quickly took three pieces and put them on my plate. Dad laughed.

"I'm not trying it, no way," Ben said adamantly.

"Good," I retorted, "then there'll be more for the rest of us."

Ben threw his napkin at me. I rolled my eyes and was about to ask if that was the best he could do, but Dad put his hand on my arm. I kept eating instead.

After lunch, Savta served cake and fruit compote. "This is such a big meal!" I blurted out in amazement, even as I helped myself to dessert.

"In Israel the main meal is eaten in the middle of the day, and dinner is much lighter," Mom explained. "Everyone comes home for a few hours in the afternoon to eat and rest, and then the adults go back to work."

"What about Saturday and Sunday?" I asked.

"People here work five and a half days a week, so it's not like our weekend."

"Five and a half days! What about kids?" Ben said, with an expression of pure horror on his face.

Mom laughed. "Guess you didn't know how good you have it."

Ben rolled his eyes. "I bet they go to school all summer too."

"No, Israeli kids have summers off just like you do. They have plenty of time to play."

"Can we go play now?" Ben asked, already out of his seat.

"Yes, go ahead."

Ben and I left the table, looking for something to do. Ben settled down to read some comic books he'd brought from home, and I wrote in my journal until I realized I was having trouble keeping my eyes open. I lay down on my cot to rest for a few minutes.

I ended up napping until supper, when Savta served the same mixture of vegetables, yogurts, and cheeses we'd seen at breakfast. We all ate together, then sat outside in the warm air. The sun set in shades of red and orange, and crickets began to chirp. While the adults talked in Hebrew, I played checkers with Ben on the front stoop until it got too dark to see the board. The first full day of our visit was coming to an end. Breathing in the smell of roses, I heard my parents' voices and felt myself relax for the first time that day.

5

The next morning Dad and I went to the supermarket to look for cereal. The woman at the cash register laughed when she saw the box and said something in Hebrew. Dad's face turned a light pink.

Afterward, as we strolled past the stores, I asked my father what the woman had said.

"I think she said we'd come a long way for a box of cereal."

"How does she know where Savta lives?"

"She doesn't. She meant the States."

"Oh. She could tell we're Americans?"

"Sure, and she thought she'd tease us a little."

"Do we really look that different?"

"Well, for starters, we're so pale we'd stick out anywhere in Israel, especially in a beach town like Nahariya. And our clothes are a little different . . .

who knows, maybe we even walk a little differently. Our box of cereal was also a giveaway. Foreigners are more likely to eat cereal for breakfast."

"But I thought you and Mom always said I was half Israeli."

"You are, because your mother is Israeli. But you were born in the United States and grew up there, so the person you are is very American. What's important is the way you feel, and I'm proud that you feel like you're half Israeli and half American. It's important to me."

We sat down on a bench. Dad held a small brown paper bag full of salted sunflower seeds. We snapped the seeds open with our teeth and ate the nuts inside. "Dad . . . I'm not sure I actually feel that way. I wish I did, but . . ." I trailed off, embarrassed. Dad nodded as if he understood.

"Being half and half isn't always easy. Your mother and I have had a very hard time over the years with our decision to stay in the States, always feeling like it somehow wasn't permanent."

I felt a sudden, sharp pain in my stomach. "It *is* permanent, isn't it?"

"Probably. I guess so," he said, laughing. "See, neither of us wants to make that definite statement, but right now it seems like we've set up our lives in New York, and that's where we're going to be." Dad looked at me and then looked away.

Later that morning, my family rode the bus to the beach. We got on at the bus stop in the square and rode through the streets of Nahariya. On the way, we passed through the center of town with its bookstores, clothing stores, and supermarket. A lot of people seemed to live in box-like houses similar to my grandparents' home, with wonderful gardens in front. The trip to the beach became a colorful flower show.

I couldn't stop thinking about that conversation with my father. I both belonged and didn't belong, and I didn't even know what it was that I might belong to. The country I'd always heard about was strange and unfamiliar. I had always felt as if Israel were some mystery in my life waiting to be solved, but I didn't have all the clues. Now I was actually here, and all I seemed to have were more questions. Who were my grandparents, really? Would I ever truly know them?

Once we were at the beach, sitting on the big blanket Mom had brought, I stared at the waves— watched them growing larger and larger until they crashed on the shore. The water crept up the sand and receded after each wave. Some children bobbed up and down in the shallow part, with the waves lifting them as if they were apples. Others dug holes deep into the sand and waited for a strong wave to wash over and fill them. The air smelled salty, and everywhere there was the sound of people talking and music playing from radios.

I spent the morning collecting tiny shells and dropping them into the glass Coke bottle I'd bought the day before. I'd begun collecting other things too and pasting them into my journal. I saved gum wrappers, bus tickets, and even toilet paper. Unlike the soft kind at home, the toilet paper here felt coarse and sort of like crepe paper. People could've easily used different colors for decorations at parties. I also pressed flowers into the book. One was a small red poppy. Another looked like a tiny pink bell.

When the sun started to feel too hot, I waded into the water to cool off. Ben joined me and we hit a beach ball back and forth. We floated up and down with the waves, swallowing salty water and getting our feet tangled in seaweed.

"Want to build a sand fort?" Ben asked after a while. Normally I considered myself too mature to play with Ben, but today I didn't mind. We headed back to shore and got to work on our fort. Children played around us, yelling to each other. Our fort had a little square tunnel cut into it to let the water in. A large wave came and doused the fort, leaving a well of water behind. A boy walked up and asked us something, pointing to the fort. Ben and I just stared up at him. He spoke again, and then turned in frustration, kicking up sand as he left.

Ben and I exchanged uneasy looks.

My father called for us to come back. It was time for lunch. Ben and I left our fort and ran up to the blanket, the hot sand burning our feet. We slipped on flip-flops and walked with our parents to the small café at the top of the sandy hill. We sat down at one of the small, round tables and Dad ordered beverages. As I dropped a thin straw into my bottle of Coke and sipped contentedly, Mom skimmed the menu. She ordered falafel, hummus, pita, and chips for all of us. I had never tasted falafel or hummus before and didn't even know what they looked like.

"They look like golf balls," Ben muttered when his sandwich arrived.

I looked into the crescent-shaped pita I held in

my hands. It was stuffed with lettuce, tomatoes, cucumbers, pickles, dark brown balls of fried something, and a white sauce. I wrinkled my nose. At least the "chips" turned out to be a large portion of French fries.

"The falafel is made of chickpeas, mashed up and fried. The sauce is called tahini. Try it, it's delicious," Mom said, taking a bite. "The hummus over there is also made from chickpeas. Tear off some bread and dunk it in."

Dad reached over to the basket of round pitas and tore off a hunk. He scooped up some hummus and popped it in his mouth.

"Terrific, just like on Allenby Street." Dad and Mom smiled at each other. Obviously, hummus and falafel had some sort of mushy meaning for them. Yuck.

I finally bit into my sandwich, dripping tahini onto the table. I took another bite, and then a few more. I tried the hummus. It was gooey but good.

"Not bad, huh?" Dad asked, a mustache of *tehina* sauce over his upper lip. "Your mom and I used to eat this for lunch almost every day."

"I like it," Ben said, dipping a wedge of pita into the hummus.

"Me too," I agreed. "Dad, tell us the story of how you and Mom met."

"Oh, you already know how we met," said Dad. "There's not much to tell. We met at Tel Aviv University when I came to Israel to study for a semester. Mom was a student there. When I went back to the States, we wrote, and I came back to visit twice. Your mother came to the States, and a while later we got married. That's all there is."

"What about the first day, the day you met?" I coaxed my father. I'd never heard those details.

"Oh, well, the first time we met was at a phone booth, believe it or not." Both Mom and Dad laughed, thinking back. "I was going to call my parents back in New York, and Mom, what were you doing?" He winked.

"I was going to call my boyfriend, but the phone was broken."

"So your mother and I were both struggling with it, trying to make it work, because there were always such horribly long lines of people waiting to make calls—"

"Then," Mom interrupted, "we gave up on the phone and started talking, and Dad walked me back to my dorm."

"But she didn't tell me where she lived, so I stood outside after we'd said good-bye, waiting to see which light would go on in the building so I could find her again."

"Then he stopped by a few days later and said he needed help with his Hebrew and did I have any free time!" Mom laughed. "I knew what he was up to the whole time."

"No, you didn't. You do now—you didn't then. Anyway, I was too shy to ask her out, so I did the next best thing."

"Right. We started having daily tutoring sessions, until your father finally asked me to the movies. It took over a month." Mom ran her hand over Dad's. "So, do you like that story?"

I giggled, feeling a little embarrassed. I thought it was very romantic, but I wasn't about to say that to Mom and Dad. Anyway, they were too busy looking at each other to notice that I hadn't answered.

I knew I'd have a lot to write in my journal that night.

6

On Thursday morning, my family traveled for four hours on three buses and finally arrived at Rivka's kibbutz. The bus dropped us off in front of a large iron gate. We walked through the entrance and up a long path past small one-story houses. Pretty gardens grew in front of most of the houses, and I spotted spiky green cactuses all around. We walked along the path for at least ten minutes until we reached a large building, which Mom told us was the dining hall.

"Is this some kind of summer camp?" Ben asked, squinting in the sun.

"No, Ben, do you remember when I explained that a kibbutz is like a farm where many people live and work together?" Mom put her hand on his shoulder.

"Yeah."

"Well, they also share everything, and part of the sharing includes eating together in the dining hall."

"All the time?"

"Every day. You'll see. We should be in time for lunch."

The dining hall was a large room full of rows and rows of long, rectangular tables. People sat at the tables in groups, eating and talking loudly. Rivka stood up from one of the tables and quickly walked over to us. As she hugged and kissed us all, a tall man with a bushy black mustache came up behind her. Mom introduced him as Yaacov, Rivka's husband. Yaacov shook my hand. He wore baggy blue pants and a faded blue shirt, both covered with splotches of dry mud.

I stared as he picked up all four of our bags at the same time and piled them in a corner. My mother gently pushed me toward a long cart where the lunch was being served.

"This is just like the school cafeteria," Ben mumbled, taking a tray from a stack near the cart. "Do people really eat here all the time?"

"Yes, and you'll see, it's a lot of fun," said Dad. "These here are fried vegetable balls. There are some carrots, and that over there looks like a potato *kugel*. We came on a good day!"

I could not in a million years understand how my father always seemed so cheerful. I needed time to get used to new places. Dad, on the other hand, was like a puppy who's always excited to greet new neighbors. This trip seemed better designed for the puppy way than my way.

I carefully balanced my tray as I walked to the table where my aunt sat. I stared at my plate and moved the food around with a fork. A boy and a girl ran up to the table, and my mother squealed. She hugged and kissed the kids and mussed their hair. She introduced the boy, Assaf, and the girl, Irit: our cousins. Irit was nine and Assaf, twelve. The four of us smiled at each other, the same uncomfortable smiles Ben and I shared with our grandparents. Assaf and Irit lingered by the table for a moment, and then ran off again, shouting something to their parents. I watched them leave the dining room. Their skin was tanned a deep brown from the sun. They wore T-shirts and shorts and no shoes. My own feet felt hot in my sneakers.

"The children need to go back to their houses, but they'll join us later at the pool," Rivka said.

Their houses? I must have looked very confused because Rivka suddenly turned to my mother and said, "Luisa, what's wrong with you? Didn't you tell them anything about the way we live?"

Mom laughed. "We're here now, they'll be able to see it. You can give them a big tour," she said sarcastically.

Rivka waved her hand at my mother as if she were brushing away an annoying fly. She turned to me. "Here, children don't sleep with their parents. They sleep with other children their own age in separate houses." Rivka raised her eyebrows at my mother. "So, where will Molly and Ben sleep tonight, in the children's houses or with you?"

"With you!" I blurted out before I could stop myself. The adults all laughed. I felt my face turn very hot; I knew it was probably beet red. Couldn't they see that even though none of this was a big deal to them, it was for me? I closed my eyes, determined not to cry in front of them. Ben came to my rescue.

"Mom said there was a pool. Where is it?"

The adults turned their attention to Ben, not even noticing I was upset. Ben chattered on, and I felt relieved and thankful. I ate my food and glanced around the dining room. Most everyone wore the same drab blue shirts and pants that Yaacov wore. While there had been children scampering around when we first arrived, now there were none. As the adults finished their meals, they carried their trays into another room and left through a door at the front of the hall.

While the adults talked in Hebrew, I wondered what Jenny, my best friend, was doing at that moment. I daydreamed about Jenny ringing the doorbell to Savta and Saba's house—she'd arrived to spend the summer with me! I imagined us swimming at the beach, eating ice cream, and whispering about the boys we'd see. Jenny would imitate the cranky bus drivers . . .

"Let's go, kids, it's time for our tour," Dad said excitedly, interrupting my daydream. Ben and I gave each other looks that said we'd better stick together.

Yaacov and Rivka spoke with each other, and then Yaacov ran off down the path.

"Yaacov will bring back our transportation," Rivka said mysteriously. She led us to a dirt road behind the dining hall.

A few minutes later Yaacov returned—riding a tractor. The tractor pulled a shallow wooden cart behind it. Rivka ushered us into the cart.

"This is great! Do you ride this around all the time?" Ben swung his arms over the side.

"The kibbutz uses it to bring people to the fields and back. Sometimes we ride it to the neighboring kibbutz to watch a movie. I'm glad you like it!"

Yaacov waved from the front of the tractor, and I laughed when he asked, "So, what do you think of my Rolls Royce?"

"Fantastic!" Dad shouted back.

Yaacov started up the tractor and we rode jerkily up the road.

Rivka pointed. "Over there behind the trees is our pool, where I think we'll spend our afternoon. It's too hot to do much else today." We rumbled down a bumpy hill. "And here is the shed where we keep our cows. Yaacov works here."

We passed the huge wooden shack. Ben pinched his nose. "Those cows really stink!" he shouted.

"You'll get used to the smell; it's not so bad after a while! We have five hundred cows. There are several more sheds like that one behind it."

"Five hundred! Wow."

"Yes, and each cow is named after a member of the kibbutz, so somewhere in there is a Yaacov cow and a Rivka cow. Irit and Assaf too. About four hundred and fifty people live on this kibbutz."

I liked the idea of naming the cows. I didn't even mind the smell so much. We continued rolling down the road, passing a large greenhouse. Rivka described the different kinds of plants that grew there. The tractor turned onto another road and drove past groves of oranges, mangoes, and sunflowers that seemed to stretch for miles. Yaacov's tractor picked up speed, and the hot wind blew my hair in my face.

"Is this really all yours?" Ben asked Rivka.

Rivka laughed. "In a way, yes. It belongs to all of us and we all take care of it." She pointed to a group of men and women picking fruit in the orange grove. "Everyone contributes what he or she can by working in some part of the kibbutz and, in return, they are given a home, food, and other things they need. The people in the laundry wash everyone's clothes, and the kitchen workers prepare all the food. Some people work in the fields, but we also have a small factory. Each member of the kibbutz has a place."

"What do you do?"

"I work two different jobs. I do some work in the greenhouse, and I also run a children's house. I'll show you the children's house when Yaacov passes near it." She pointed to a group of buildings off in the distance. "That's our neighbor, another kibbutz. Our children go to school together."

The tractor swung around a corner and down a rocky hill. A row of small white houses stood off to the side. I could see the dining hall a short distance away.

"Here is our guest house, where you'll all stay tonight," Rivka said, patting my hair. "Your parents could probably use some time to get settled. Would you kids like to see the children's house where I work?"

"Okay," I answered. Rivka smiled often, and it made me feel welcome.

"Ben?"

"Sure," he said, shrugging his shoulders.

"The children in my house are little, so they'll probably be napping, but we might catch a devil or two awake."

Ben and I climbed out of the cart and followed Rivka up a stone path. She led us past a playground and into another small house. Inside, a woman ironed clothing.

"My niece and nephew from America," Rivka told the woman in English. "Ben and Molly, this is Dalia. We work here together."

Dalia said hello and then whispered something to Rivka in Hebrew.

"Dalia said the children were monsters today and just fell asleep, so we're not to disturb them, but we can still take a look. Follow me."

Rivka brought us into the room, where four children slept peacefully in small cribs.

"How old are they?" Ben whispered.

"Two, two and a half."

"They're cute," I said softly.

"We can come back later and play. We'd better go now."

As we walked out of the children's house, Rivka put her arms around us.

"Why don't we sit down for a moment and talk a little? Your parents are probably taking naps of their own by now anyway."

We sat cross-legged on the thick grass in front of the children's house. I thought I heard the faint sound of cows mooing.

"Don't those little kids miss their moms and dads?" Ben asked hesitantly. "Don't their parents miss them?"

"It's different from what you're used to, I know. But except for when they're sleeping, we see the children quite a lot. They pop into the dining hall at lunchtime. And in the evening, after their parents have finished work, we all have dinner in the dining hall and spend time together until the children get ready for bed. It's just a different way of doing things."

"But why can't they sleep with you?" I asked.

"Well, the idea for children to sleep apart came about a long time ago, back when all the members of a new kibbutz, men and women, needed to work very long hours to keep the kibbutz running. That would have been very hard on the children, to have to adjust to that kind of schedule. The separate houses meant that one person could watch over a group of children, making sure they were well taken care of while their parents worked. Of course, things are different now—1986 is not 1948. Many *kibbutzim* have begun to change and have children sleep with their parents in their apartments. We might do that here one day. People talk about it." Rivka pulled several blades of grass out of the ground and tickled Ben's nose. "Now it's your turn: tell me about what you like to do. Tell me about where you live."

It was easy to talk to Rivka. We told her about our friends and our neighborhood, the apartment we lived in, and the school we went to every day.

I described Bubbe, whom Rivka remembered but not that well. Ben talked about his baseball team and the run he'd scored the last week of the season. When I pointed out that it was his *only* run, he poked me in the ribs.

Just as Ben was talking about his part in the school play, Assaf and Irit ran up to us. They said something to Rivka, and she looked at her watch, cringing.

"Well, kids, we were supposed to meet these two and your uncle Yaacov at the pool forty-five minutes ago. As you can see, they've been waiting. But I'm glad we had a chance to talk. Now let's go—get your bathing suits!"

Ben and I sprinted to our parents' room and returned a few minutes later with our suits on. We reported that our parents were in fact sleeping, just like Rivka's babies. The five of us walked across the kibbutz to the pool, where we spotted Yaacov relaxing on a lawn chair.

"Did you get lost?" he asked Rivka, squinting in the sun and smiling.

"A little."

We four kids sat on the grass near Rivka and Yaacov. I felt the familiar uneasy feeling as I looked over at my cousins. How would I ever talk to them?

Rivka said something to Irit in Hebrew, and she ran off to a small shed behind the pool, returning with a beach ball.

"Okay, everybody in the water!" Rivka repeated what she said in Hebrew. We all jumped in the water, and Rivka began batting the ball around to each of us. Soon enough, an informal volleyball game began, kids against adults. Assaf purposely hit the ball short of his father, splashing him. This set off a battle between the two sides to see who could splash whom the hardest. Every time I was the target I laughed; it felt great. Yaacov blasted me over and over again. The game ended when an elderly woman sitting by the pool got an unexpected shower and yelled at us to stop.

After a few laps around the pool, we all returned to our grassy spot to wrap ourselves in towels and dry off in the still-hot afternoon sun. My parents appeared at the gate to the entrance of the pool.

"Hi!" Dad shouted across. "We're going for a walk."

"I know where they're going," Rivka said. "She's showing him the grapevine. It's our own lovers' lane, a good place for a secret kiss."

I wrinkled my nose.

"No, not your parents!" Rivka teased.

"Rivka," Ben interrupted, "if we lived in Israel, would we live here?"

"Hmm, probably not. Your parents are more suited to the city. They would be teachers here like they are in New York, but I don't think they would choose to live on a kibbutz."

"How come you live here?"

By this time Assaf and Irit had drawn closer, curious to know what we were talking about. Yaacov translated the conversation into Hebrew so they could understand.

"I came to this kibbutz when I was in the army," Rivka explained. "I joined a special group that serves part of its years of duty on kibbutzim. I had always lived in small towns with my parents, but I came here and I liked it. Then I met Yaacov, who has lived here all his life, and, well, you can pretty much see the rest." Rivka ran her hand through Irit's hair.

"How come you speak English?" Ben asked.

"I learned in school, and so did Yaacov. In a few years the children will learn English too."

"What about Saba and Savta?"

"Well, they've spoken Romanian or Yiddish most of their lives. When they came to Israel, they needed to learn Hebrew. They've never had the opportunity to learn English."

Assaf said something to Yaacov. Yaacov hesitated, and then spoke to us. "Assaf thinks the two of you should speak Hebrew. He doesn't think Saba or Savta will be learning any English."

Neither Ben nor I said anything. A small part of me was angry with Assaf for saying what he had, but a bigger part knew that Assaf was absolutely right. If I wanted to get to know my grandparents, I would have to figure out a way to communicate with them.

But how?

And with just twenty-five days left, did I even have enough time?

During dinner in the dining hall, lots of people from the kibbutz stopped by our long table to meet us. Some sat down with us, drinking a cup of coffee or picking at a platter of fruit Rivka had placed in the center of the table. Some people asked me a few questions in English; others didn't talk to me at all. I wasn't sure which I preferred. My mother talked with everyone, laughing a lot. I noticed that Dad was quiet most of the time, and when he did speak, it was in the same halting way I'd first heard him speak Hebrew to my grandmother.

After dinner, we all went to Rivka and Yaacov's home for dessert. They lived in a small one-story house, and when I walked through the door I was surprised by all the color on the white walls. I touched the fabrics hanging alongside dozens of framed photographs and shelves full of books and plants. Ben and I picked out our mother in several photographs and even found some pictures of ourselves.

From the kitchen, Rivka brought platters full of fruit, nuts, and squares of cake. Coffee brewed in a pot, and she offered us kids cups of hot chocolate.

Assaf and Irit brought out a game—backgammon. We took turns playing while the adults talked to each other. After several games Irit rolled her eyes and said something to me. I didn't understand and shrugged. Irit pointed to a closet and waved her hand for me to follow her as she walked into it and began rummaging around. Irit pulled out a photo album and led me into the bedroom, leaving the boys behind to play another round.

Irit and I sat on the bed, and Irit opened the large album on her lap. She pointed at the first photograph: a young couple, dressed as if they were going to a party, their elbows linked together. "Savta and Saba," Irit said. "Romania." I realized that the photo had been taken before Israel, before World War II, before our mothers had been born.

We paused on each page of the book. Irit pointed at the black-and-white photographs and told me the names and the places. The family in Romania, then in Israel, first in tents and then a small house. I had seen similar pictures in my mother's photo album at home, but I had never really thought about them. What had it been like for her to grow up in Romania and to come to Israel when she was so young?

We came to a photo of two little girls, their hair in braids. "Your mother and my mother, Rivka and Luisa." Irit spoke in Hebrew, but I understood.

As Irit turned the pages, my mother and Rivka became young girls, then teenagers. These were photographs I'd never seen and I looked at them intently. Irit tapped her finger on a picture of her mother in an army uniform. There was a series of these photographs, mostly with Rivka surrounded by other young people dressed in uniforms and smiling. Then there were pictures of the kibbutz, and Yaacov. Rivka and Yaacov's wedding. Pictures of camping trips, parties, holidays. A photograph of Rivka on Yaacov's shoulders and then Rivka with a large, round belly. Dozens of pictures of Assaf, followed by just as many of Irit. Assaf and Irit grew up in the photographs too, and the pictures became full of color. We both laughed when we flipped past one of Assaf as a toddler sitting on the back of a large cow.

I giggled at the pictures of myself that popped up now and again. I pointed at my father's heavy black-rimmed glasses, my mother's frizzy hairdo, and my own jumper with the huge, multicolored flowers. Irit laughed with me.

Savta and Saba were in a lot of the pictures, holding the children or celebrating a holiday. Irit spoke the familiar names—Sukkot, Purim, Pesach. There were photos of Savta and Saba with the kids in the sukkah, the branches overhead letting in light. Irit dressed up as Princess Leia and Assaf as Spiderman for Purim. Irit leaning against Savta and holding up a piece of matzah on Passover. These were my holidays too, and I celebrated them with my parents, and with Bubbe, at home and at our synagogue. But now something occurred to me that I'd never thought of before. In some alternate universe, I would have been in those pictures too. Eating matzah. Dressing up for Purim. Lighting the menorah at Hanukkah. Me, sitting with Savta and Saba, laughing.

Weird.

I felt like I had missed out on something. Not that I would ever want to give up my own memories, but . . . Why did I know one part of my family and not the other?

After a while we closed the album and rejoined the group in the other room, snatching up chunks of marble sponge cake on our way. Our mothers were talking in Hebrew, loudly.

Shouting.

Mom's cheeks were red, and Assaf and Ben had stopped their game to stare at them. Yaacov stood up and walked over to the kitchen, and I edged up to him.

"Why are they shouting?" I whispered.

"They're arguing politics." He winked. "Your mother and sister never agree on politics. But I think they just love to argue."

They didn't look like they were enjoying themselves, but then again, my mother did like discussing politics. Suddenly Mom turned to Dad, who had been glancing from her to Rivka, trying to keep up with the conversation.

"David, tell her," she said in English. "You know more about this country's history than she does."

My father opened his mouth as if to say something, then stopped.

"I don't need David to remind me about my own history, thank you very much," snapped Rivka.

"I think you do. You obviously have no idea

how dangerous it would be to give back all that land. David . . ."

"Don't tell me what it would mean. I know exactly what it will mean, and why it has to be done. I live here. My children live here. Don't tell me that I don't know when you don't even live here!"

Rivka leaned back into the couch. Everyone was very quiet. Tears rolled down Rivka's cheeks. My mother stood up and walked out of the house.

Dad rubbed his chin. "Rivka . . ."

"I'm sorry, David," Rivka said, wiping her eyes with her sleeve. "I ruined our evening."

"No, you didn't. I hope the two of you will get a chance to talk. Kids, I'll be right back."

After he'd followed Mom outside, Ben and I looked at each other but no one said anything. I bit my nails.

"Does anyone want anything?" Rivka asked. "No? Okay."

Assaf spoke to his mother in Hebrew, and she answered him. Then she turned to Ben and me. "Assaf wanted to know what we fought about. We were arguing about the occupied territories and what should happen to them, and different ideas people have about peace, and if it can really come to us. But

I think we were also fighting because . . . we live very different lives and don't always agree with each other's decisions. But I hope you know how glad I am that you're here now. I just want to get to know you as much as possible."

I didn't know what the territories were, or what decisions Rivka was talking about. I knew I'd have to ask my father later.

Rivka picked up the plates and leftover food and brought it all into the kitchen. The rest of us sat restlessly on the floor of the living room. Assaf stacked backgammon pieces into a small tower, but no one made a move to play.

"I have an idea," Yaacov announced, then translated. "Follow me." Ben and I looked at each other and then followed Yaacov out the door, with Assaf and Irit trailing behind.

Outside, it was very dark, and I stared up at a sky specked with more stars than I'd ever seen. The moon was large and round. We followed Yaacov through the kibbutz, all the way to the pool. Several lights shone on the water, making it glisten. I looked up at Yaacov and he smiled down at me.

"Have you ever taken a swim at night, under the stars?"

I shook my head.

"Well, then . . ." Yaacov kicked off his shoes. "Now would be a good time!" And then he jumped in, with all his clothes on, right into the deep end. Assaf and Irit followed him. I slipped off my sneakers and stuck one foot into the water. It was warm! Ben jumped in, and then I did too.

"Good?" Yaacov asked.

"It's great!" Ben and I shouted, echoing each other.

"This is something our teenagers love to do, especially on birthdays. Almost everyone gets thrown in once, usually when they're half asleep."

Irit climbed onto her father's back, linking her arms under his chin.

I floated on my back, looking up to the sky, the stars, and the moon, feeling calm again. I'd never seen my mother leave a room in the middle of a conversation, even if it was a fight. And Rivka had cried. Was the fight over, or had it just begun?

After a while Yaacov told us it was time to get out of the water. Suddenly it didn't seem as warm outside anymore, and we shivered in our soaking wet clothes.

"Let's run back!" Yaacov suggested, and we

dashed after him through the kibbutz, carrying our shoes and socks.

Back at the house, Rivka and Mom were sitting and hugging on the couch. Both of them looked like they'd been crying. When they saw us, Rivka's mouth dropped open.

"Yaacov, are you crazy? Look at these children!" She ran to the closet and grabbed a bunch of towels, wrapping one around each of our dripping bodies.

"You *are* crazy," she told her husband, shaking her head. "I thought you were bringing the children back to their houses." Yaacov kissed her on the cheek.

"Well, did you have fun swimming?" Mom asked us.

"Yeah!" Ben said. "I think it's better than swimming during the day."

Dad walked up to me and put his hands on my shoulders. "All right, time for bed. It's been a long day. Luisa?"

"I think I'll stay a while." Mom gave Ben a kiss on his forehead. "Sleep well." She kissed me too, and toweled my hair a bit. "You okay?"

"Yeah," I said. "Are you?"

"Yes, sweetie. Rivka and I are having a good

talk, one we probably should have had a long time ago. I'm sorry you saw us shouting at each other."

I hugged my mother, and she hugged me back tightly.

● ● ●

Later, when we were tucked into our cots at the guesthouse, I whispered, "Dad, what are the territories? Rivka said something about them."

He sighed. "The territories. Well, it's not easy to explain. There are sections of land that Israel has held since the Six-Day War in 1967. These areas are very important to many Jews because they contain holy places and are part of ancient Israel. At the same time, the territories are home to many Palestinians who want to have their own nation. The land is important to them too. Both Israelis and Palestinians want to claim their own layer of history. And that's partly why there's been so much fighting. Some Israelis want to give up the territories, in the hope that Palestinian independence will lead to peace. Other people feel that this would lead to more violence. Your mother and her sister disagree."

"What do you think?" Ben asked.

"It's very difficult, Ben. I want the violence to stop, but it's very hard to know how that will happen. Maybe eventually some kind of solution will be reached by the two sides talking."

I listened to the crickets outside, chirping, and soon I heard Ben's slow way of breathing that let me know he was asleep. I drifted off thinking about something being so special that everyone would want a part of it—and be willing to fight for it.

8

When I woke up the next morning, I heard tractors outside and water running in the bathroom. I glanced over to my parents' bed and saw Mom asleep, a pillow pulled over her head.

My father emerged from the bathroom, spots of shaving cream still dotting his chin. He woke Ben, and the three of us dressed silently, tiptoeing around the room so we wouldn't wake Mom. We went to the dining hall and served ourselves a breakfast of vegetables and hard-boiled eggs. Soon Mom joined us, looking sleepy but more relaxed than she'd seemed in a while.

"What time did you come back last night?" Ben asked her.

"I don't know. Late. I think it was actually morning."

"You and Rivka talked all that time?" I asked.

"Yes. We had a lot of important things to talk about. So, once we started, we just kept talking and talking . . ."

"About the territories?"

"The territories?" For a moment she looked confused. She glanced over at Dad. "No, about each other. We had a lot of catching up to do."

Ben sprinkled salt on his egg. "Are you still mad at each other?"

"No, Ben, we're not. Sometimes when Rivka and I get angry with each other we hold it in, and sometimes we need to let it out. We're glad we finally talked about some of the things that were bothering both of us. We feel very differently about some things, and maybe we always will, but I hope you won't see us fight that way again."

"What things do you always fight about?" I pressed.

My mother chewed on a slice of pepper. "Rivka . . . was very angry for a long time when I moved away, and when I didn't bring you here, until now. And I was always angry with her . . . I guess because she was angry with me, and I sometimes wondered about the decisions I made too. I also hadn't thought the kibbutz was the right place for her when she chose it."

"Where did you want her to live? In the city?"

"I just wanted her to continue with school. Rivka was a very good student. I wanted her to go to college. I thought she would grow up to be a chemist, or a doctor, or . . ."

"A teacher," Dad said. "Like you."

For a moment, my mother looked uncomfortable. "I suppose. I suppose that's true." She stared out the window. "And she could have pursued all sorts of careers and still lived on the kibbutz. But it turns out that this is what makes her happy." She turned back to us with a shrug. "Anyway, let's talk about what we're doing this morning. We'll need to catch the bus right after lunch to get back to Nahariya in time for Shabbat."

We agreed on a short swim, and in no time we were splashing each other and diving for coins in the shallow end of the kibbutz pool. I was happy when Rivka appeared at the pool's edge and dipped a toe into the water.

"Are you coming to swim with us?" Ben asked.

"No, I'm just taking a break. I have to go back to the children, but I wanted to come and say hello.

This is the last day I'll see you before Meir's wedding." She exchanged some words with Mom in Hebrew, and I thought they looked more at ease with each other than they had since we'd arrived.

"Does anyone want to come for a visit with the little ones?"

"I do!" I answered. "I'd love to see them." I climbed out of the pool, pulled a T-shirt over my bathing suit, and followed Rivka. Just a few days ago, I might have hesitated to go off alone with a relative I didn't know. But Rivka had a way of making me feel comfortable, as if she'd always been a part of my life.

We found the children playing outside in a small playground with miniature swings, slides, and a sandbox. Plastic toys were strewn all over the grass. Dalia scolded a child who had just spilled a pail of sand over another boy's head.

"Two and a half and already a bully," Rivka said. "He reminds me of an old story about someone in our family."

"Really? Who?"

"I'll tell you in a minute." She spoke with Dalia briefly, then turned back to me.

"Okay, Dalia would like us to help with the

laundry, and she'll watch the kids. Then it will be our turn. Let's go."

We went inside the small house and began folding clothes out of a large hamper. Rivka sorted each child's clothes according to the Hebrew letters stenciled into the collar or waistband.

"So, what's the story?" I asked.

"It's about your grandfather's brothers, a long time ago when they were boys in Romania. Have you heard all the old stories a million times already?"

"Only a few," I said quietly. "I'd love to know more."

"Well, your grandfather had six brothers and sisters, and they were always getting into trouble. One of the brothers, whose Hebrew name is Yehezkel, was four years old and still didn't speak. This is quite unusual, and his parents took him to many doctors, but no reason or cause could be found. The next son, Itzhak, was two and a half, and your Saba hadn't been born yet.

"Anyway, one day your great-grandmother is cooking in her kitchen and Yehezkel runs in, his head bleeding, with Itzhak right behind him. Of course, Yehezkel was rushed to the doctor, who cleaned him up. Later, when the household calmed down, their mother investigated what had happened. I still remember her telling me how little Itzhak finally spoke up in his small voice and said, 'But Mama, Yehezkel wasn't polite. I asked him a question and he wouldn't answer!' So he'd hit Yehezkel in the head with a brick." Rivka shook her head. "Children . . . Anyway, three or four weeks later Yehezkel started talking, in full sentences and very opinionated, as if he'd been doing it all along. It was a happy ending for a story involving a brick."

"That's funny! I'm glad it has a happy ending."

"Yes, that's one of the stories that does."

"Are they still alive, Yehezkel and Itzhak?" I asked.

"Yes, those two as well as another brother and sister of Saba's are still alive. You'll meet them soon, I'm sure."

"I know I'm named after his sister Malka."

Rivka nodded. "That made Saba very happy."

We'd finished all the laundry, leaving six neat piles on the table. I scratched an itch at the back of my neck. "What was Malka like?"

"Malka died young, from pneumonia. I've heard she was very sweet, very creative. Saba said she used to make up games to keep all the little children busy."

"What else?"

"I don't know a lot about her. Maybe we can ask Saba to tell us more."

"Okay," I said. "I'd like that." I paused. "You'll have to help me talk to him."

"I will, but you know, Molly, you'll also need to try on your own. Your mother told me it's been hard for everyone. You have to try, because otherwise you won't feel completely comfortable."

Try? I was trying! My head felt like it was going to explode. Why did everyone seem to think not speaking Hebrew was somehow my fault?

I felt my cheeks getting hot again, not from embarrassment this time, but from anger. "But I don't understand them! How can I talk to them?"

"You don't have to talk. Just be with them. If you can begin to feel comfortable with them, then communication will come. I saw you last night with Irit. You were fine, Molly."

Rivka put two fingers under my chin, lifting my head slightly. "Have confidence in yourself, and it won't seem as hard. Want to go see the children now?"

It was hard to stay mad at Rivka, so I smiled and nodded. And anyway, she had a point. Her words repeated in my head like music. A song I wanted to remember.

Outside, the children were still playing, with Dalia mediating small arguments and tugs-of-war. Rivka shooed Dalia off to her break, leaving us alone with the four toddlers. At first I tentatively sat in the corner of the sandbox, watching. Soon a little girl pushed a ball my way, and I rolled it back. Next thing I knew, another toddler sat beside me. The girl made patties out of sand and water, and invited another boy to join us. We sat in a circle and took imaginary bites. I knew how to play tea party, of course. I got by with the simple words I knew—*ken* was "yes"; *lo* meant "no." Turns out you can get pretty far with pointing.

Soon we were all sitting in the sandbox, mixing sand and water batters for cookies and cakes, and generally making a mess. Rivka helped with some words. The way Rivka smiled at me made me feel like this visit, and maybe the whole trip, was turning out all right after all.

When Dalia came back, Rivka and I left to meet everyone in the dining hall. We stopped off first at the guest room, where I changed my clothes and packed my bag.

"It's great having guests," Rivka said, stretching out on the bed. "I don't have to work too hard!"

I laughed. "Do you like it here?"

"Living here? Yes, I like it very much."

"It seems like a nice place to live."

"It is. But it's not for everyone."

"What do you like about it?"

"Hmmm . . . many, many things. I like living on a farm. I like that our children have so much space to run around. I like all the smells, the animals, the stars at night," Rivka said, and then laughed. "Sounds funny, right?"

"It sounds good." We'd left the room, heading for the dining hall.

"Everyone has to find their own place. I spent a lot of time thinking about what was right for me. So did your mother. We were lucky to have so many choices."

I couldn't help wondering about the choices my mother had made, and whether Mom felt they'd been the right ones.

Over lunch with the rest of the family, Rivka and I described the games we'd played with the children. Irit and Assaf talked about their morning visit to a neighboring kibbutz and the friends they'd seen. Rivka translated and also taught us some new words in English and Hebrew.

Chaver means "friend."

9

My family reached Savta and Saba's house tired and hungry. *We've only been gone a day,* I thought, *but it feels like so much happened.* When I saw Savta I did the first thing that popped into my head and kissed her on the cheek. Savta looked surprised.

We had arrived just in time for sundown and the beginning of Shabbat. We all gathered around the kitchen table. It looked different covered with a long, white tablecloth and set with fancy dishes. A large loaf of challah sat at one end. Mom ran into the kitchen, put a scarf over her head, and whispered a prayer as she lit two candles.

Saba sang the prayer over the wine, and we each had a taste. After he said the prayer over the challah, he tore off thick pieces of the bread and sprinkled them with salt, passing them around to the family.

The prayers were familiar to me. Whether we were in New York or here in Israel, Friday nights were the same.

We ate a long, slow dinner of fish, chicken soup, chicken and vegetables, and a dessert of fruits and cake. Mom and Dad chatted with my grandparents in Hebrew. At first Ben and I were quiet, but slowly, we also began to join in the conversation.

"Tell them about the tractor ride," Ben said. "Has Yaacov ever driven them on one?"

Mom spoke in Hebrew, and Savta and Saba chuckled. They answered, and we heard the translation.

"Savta and Saba are glad you got a chance to tour the kibbutz in a tractor. And no, they've never been on one." Our mother smiled.

"Did you tell them I played with Rivka's babies?" I added. Mom translated.

"Tell them about how we swam at night in the pool!" Ben exclaimed.

"I don't think so," Mom said. "Some things we keep to ourselves."

I already missed Rivka and the others. I wished we didn't have to wait until Meir's wedding—the very end of our trip—to spend more time with them.

"Hey, when is Meir going to visit us again?" Ben asked between mouthfuls of cake.

"Meir is in the army right now, in reserves. He was called for two weeks of duty. He got a pass to come see us the night we arrived."

"I thought he was a sculpture, not a soldier," Ben said.

"A sculptor. In Israel, every sculptor is a soldier," Dad answered. He helped himself to a fig and another slice of cake.

"Most men and women in Israel join the army when they turn eighteen," Mom explained. "Some people are excused, but most serve."

"So if we lived here, Molly and I would go into the army too?"

"Right. Men go for three years, women for two. Then men typically serve in the reserves until they're fifty. They're called up for a few weeks every year."

"Meir had to go even though he's getting married in two weeks?" I asked incredulously.

"That's right. Luckily he'll be finished in a few days. Then we'll visit him in Tel Aviv. He's promised us a great time."

"What's his fiancée like?" I wondered aloud.

"I'm looking forward to meeting her myself. I've heard many lovely things about her from Meir. I met some of Meir's other girlfriends, but he met Ma'ayan after the last time I was here. Mama . . ." With that, my mother spoke a string of Hebrew words to Savta, then listened to her response.

"Well, Savta says to tell you she's very nice. Hmm? Oh, and Saba says she's very pretty and laughs a lot. Rivka said she was young."

"How young?"

"Well, ten years younger than Meir, but then, that's my brother!" Mom and Dad laughed.

I found all this information intriguing. Meir, for one thing, sounded quite interesting. But how did my mother feel, having never met the person Meir was about to marry?

Savta got up from the table and returned with a photograph. In it, Meir stood with his arm around a slight woman with long, red hair. "Ma'ayan," Savta said, after she'd handed the photograph to me.

"Ma'ayan is a folk dancer. That's all I really know," Mom said with a sigh, and I knew the answer to my question.

That night we all sat outside. The garden smelled of overripe fruit and roses. On Shabbat, my grandparents didn't watch television or listen to the radio. Small nightlights were plugged into sockets, and the kitchen light would shine all night long. This way of observing the Sabbath was new to me. At home we turned lights on and off, and our parents drove their car.

"Does everyone observe Shabbat like this here?" Ben asked.

"No," Mom answered. "Some people don't at all. But many people do. The buses won't run until after Shabbat is over, but some movie theaters are open for people who want to go."

Out of respect for our grandparents, Mom asked that we not write or watch television or turn on lights until after Shabbat was over.

"But what *can* we do?" Ben asked. He and I sat side by side on the stoop.

"You can do a lot. When I was growing up, I loved Shabbat. It was such a special time. There was no homework, no work to do in the house, nothing but free time to play together."

"What would you do?"

"We read a lot, or played games, or took walks to explore the neighborhood. The family visited, and our cousins would come to play. Someone would bring a movie magazine, or we would tell stories. Sometimes we made up plays, arguing about the characters and the costumes for hours. We would make a theater in the garden and perform for our parents. They always loved it . . ." She leaned back in her chair and stared up at the sky.

"Sounds fun. Why didn't you ever tell us about that before?" Ben asked.

Mom shrugged. "I don't know."

I watched my mother stand up and walk over to the small tray of fruit Savta had brought outside. She absentmindedly picked a grape and rolled it between her fingers.

"Mom?"

She turned around to look at me.

"Tell us more stories," I said.

My mother nodded. "I'll try . . . I really will," she said gently.

We sat outside until the warm wind and steady rhythm of the crickets lulled us into quiet thought-fulness. Later on, lying in my bed, I stared up at the shadows on the ceiling and thought of my mother as a young girl, making up plays and telling stories. We were more alike than I had ever realized.

10

When we woke the next day, there was none of the usual morning noise outside. The streets were silent. Saba returned from synagogue and sat down with us for breakfast. He pinched my cheek softly and spoke to my parents.

"What did he say?" I asked.

"He told everyone at the synagogue about the two of you," Mom explained. "The rabbi gave him a special honor today in celebration of our reunion."

"What kind of honor?"

"Saba was invited to read from the Torah."

I looked at my grandfather, and he smiled back, his eyes shining from behind his round eyeglasses. When he spoke, he looked right at me and Ben, and Mom echoed him in English.

"Saba said that some of our relatives will come to

visit this afternoon. He saw them in synagogue this morning. He says he can't wait to show you off."

Ben and I both smiled. Savta carried a small bag of garbage to the metal barrel outside. As soon as she was out of sight, Saba stood up and walked quickly into another room. He returned with a box, opening it to reveal rows of chocolates.

"*Abba!*" Mom exclaimed. She seemed to scold him, but he just waved his hand at her and offered us the candy. Dad grinned and said nothing.

"Fine, have chocolate for breakfast," sighed Mom. "That's exactly what he would do when we were children, and *my* mother would always yell. I must be getting old!"

"Yehoshua!" Savta had returned from outside and we all burst out laughing at the sight of Savta frowning at Saba.

"Some things never change," said Mom with a smile.

• • •

Later that morning, I wandered into Saba and Savta's bedroom and looked again at the photograph on the wall. I called to my mother.

"What?" Mom asked, walking in.

"Tell me about this picture," I said, pointing to the photograph.

"Hmmm. That's Savta, and Saba, and Savta's brother Herschel with his wife Etti. Here I am, and baby Meir and Rivka, and my cousins, Baruch and Yehudit. This picture was taken a few days before we all left Romania on the boat to Israel."

"Everyone looks so sad."

"Yes, well, we were excited to be coming to Israel, but it was hard to leave, not really knowing what to expect. The years after the war had been very difficult, almost as hard as the war itself had been, and everyone knew we would need to leave. I was born in '47—two years after the end of the war, right before Israel became a state. We came here in 1953, I think. I don't remember much of it."

We sat down on the bed. "What did Savta and Saba do during the war?"

"They were scared, mostly. In the end, they were very lucky. The Russians took over their town before the Nazis could get to them. Saba was taken to a work camp for a year and then released. But if the Russians hadn't come, things could have been much worse, as they were for other Jews in Europe."

"They could have been sent to concentration camps?"

"Yes. They lived in fear and prayed. I guess the Russians were the answer to their prayers, but when the war ended, the Russians didn't treat the Jews well either. Saba and Herschel planned how to bring the families here and finally got visas. So Israel was the real answer to their prayers. Herschel and Etti live close by. They'll come to visit this afternoon."

"What about Baruch and Yehudit?"

"Yehudit is married to a man named Amir. They have a son, Erez, and don't live far from here." Mom was silent for a moment. "Baruch died, Molly, fighting in the Yom Kippur War here in 1973. I can't believe it's been thirteen years since then. Ben is named after him. He was a wonderful man, very gentle and kind, and a great storyteller." She paused and then smiled. "We made up all those Shabbat plays together."

I leaned my head on my mother's shoulder, and Mom put her arm around me.

"Did Savta and Saba ever want to come to the United States to live with us?" I asked.

"No. This is the only home for them."

I looked up at my mother. She was staring out the window.

"You know, Molly, this isn't an easy place to live, but it is a special place. It really is a special place."

I knew that Israel was special to many people, but what I was most curious about was why it was special to my mother, and why she'd practically kept it to herself, like a secret. I was about to ask the question when Mom stood up, saying she heard people coming up the steps.

I followed her, lagging behind. She opened the screen door to shouts and squeals that reminded me of our arrival at the airport. Before I knew it, I'd been grabbed into a big hug and crushed against a woman's chest.

"*Maideleh!*" the woman crooned, and I remembered how Bubbe would also use that Yiddish term of affection with me. Ben and I met Herschel and Etti, plus Yehudit and her husband. Then there were Esther and Avraham and Rahel and Moshe, Savta's sisters and their husbands, who also lived here in Nahariya. I quickly tried to memorize all the new names. I couldn't believe I had so many relatives.

The new arrivals created an instant party. The adults talked all at once—and loudly. Dad tried to help Ben and me understand what everyone was saying. Savta served sweets and coffee, pouring hot water out of thermoses she kept for Shabbat. The adults drizzled liquor over slices of cake. Then gifts were exchanged: Mom passed out the presents she had brought, and Ben and I found ourselves holding brightly wrapped packages from our relatives. I unwrapped a beaded necklace, a wall hanging like the ones in Rivka's home, and a pack of cards with different pictures of Jerusalem on each one.

"*Todah, todah,*" I said, using the word for "thank you" I'd learned in Hebrew school.

Yehudit spoke English and told us about Erez, explaining that he'd recently begun the army and wasn't always home for Shabbat. She passed around a photograph of a group of soldiers. "This is Erez with all the kids from his class," Yehudit said.

I remembered what our parents had told us about all Israelis serving in the army. I was busy imagining myself in a khaki uniform when there was a loud knock at the door. Savta went to see who it was, and when she reappeared, a man in that exact uniform stood behind her.

"Erez!" Yehudit shouted, and then a garble of Hebrew followed, with everyone jumping up to hug him. Erez smiled sheepishly as his relatives ran their fingers through his crew-cut hair and slapped him on the back.

"Hello," he said to Ben and me when we were introduced. "I couldn't let my cousins come all the way from America and not stop by to say hello," he added, beaming.

We spent the rest of the afternoon chewing on candies and cake and listening to the relatives exchange news. Dad did his best to translate what he could, and occasionally Erez added in the translation himself.

"I was just telling them about an Ethiopian guy in my group," Erez said. "He wants to be a paratrooper like me, and he received honors last week."

"He's from Ethiopia?" I asked.

"There are many Ethiopians here, Jews who came to Israel a couple of years ago in a big airlift," Dad explained. "They came with their own Jewish traditions that they'd practiced for centuries."

Esther spoke, and Erez translated. "She says that a few years ago she was sitting in a café with a friend when she saw two men meet on the street. They were very excited to see each other. As she watched, one man kissed the other, once on the nose, on the cheek, on the forehead—maybe six different places!

She asked her friend what they were doing, and she explained that Ethiopians kiss each other once for each year they have been apart."

"I like that story," I said.

"So, maybe I give you twelve kisses?" Esther said haltingly, and then laughed and kissed me once on the cheek.

The stories kept coming, covering news from each part of the family. I sat cross-legged on the floor and listened. Yehudit was looking for a new job. Rahel's neighbor had just flown to Argentina to visit relatives. Yehudit said that Erez had a new girlfriend, and Erez blushed. They talked about Meir's wedding, about politics, about the weather, and then, to my horror, they began to talk about us. Some of the stories were funny, some were embarrassing, and some were from so long ago that I didn't remember them myself.

Ben rolled his eyes as Mom described a particularly embarrassing episode that involved Ben and a certain cowboy costume. "Can't we talk about something else?"

"Don't worry," Erez said with a wink. "You're a big kid now. But your mother does love that story. I think she tells it every time she visits!"

Ben groaned.

"I do not," my mother protested, but when Erez repeated what he'd said in Hebrew, everyone in the room nodded and laughed.

The guests stayed all afternoon, until Moshe fell asleep in his chair, his snores making everyone laugh. Rahel nudged him awake with her elbow. Then they all gathered at the door and said good-bye, hugging and kissing and promising to see each other the following Shabbat.

And as for me? It had been an afternoon of new people and stories and food and laughter. I'd had a great time.

11

Dear Bubbe,

We've spent the last few days at the beach and going on day trips. Yesterday we visited a place called Rosh Hanikra. We rode in cable cars up to huge caverns where the ocean crashed against the rocks. Then we stood on a cliff and peered over the border into Lebanon. Dad told us about the war that happened there not long ago. It was hard to imagine. Today it was quiet, but Israeli soldiers were everywhere. I saw United Nations peacekeepers in blue helmets too. It made me think how different it is to live here, in ways I would've never thought about at home. I've taken a lot for granted.

● ● ●

I woke up Thursday morning to the sound of raised voices coming from my grandparents' room. I tiptoed across the cool stone floor of the hallway to listen at the door. Hebrew. Or was it Romanian?

I peered into the room. Saba, Savta, and my mother seemed to be arguing. Mom was holding Saba's pants, and he was trying to pull them away from her. He stood in the middle of the room in his pajamas.

"Molly, go back to bed. It's very early," my mother said sternly when she spotted me in the doorway. Savta shooed me away.

I went to the kitchen to look at the clock. Five thirty in the morning. On my way back to bed Dad passed me, already dressed and rushing to the front door.

"What's going on? Where are you going?" I called to him.

"Saba's sick. It's nothing serious, just a cold. I'm going to tend the store for him. You and Ben can come help me later. It'll be fun." With that, he was gone.

I crawled back into bed. I found it a bit hard to imagine my father behind the wooden table in the fish store. It was even harder to imagine myself being of any help to him. I thought about the gray fish nudging each other in the tank, and slowly fell back asleep.

When I woke up again a few hours later, the house was quiet. Ben was still asleep. I dressed and walked around the house looking for my mother, but I couldn't find her anywhere. I stopped at the door to my grandparents' room. Saba was lying in bed, reading the newspaper. He looked up at me and smiled.

"Shalom, Saba," I said.

"Shalom, Molly," he answered. I liked the way my grandfather pronounced my name: "Mo-lee."

"Ima?" I asked, hoping he would understand.

"Ima, Abba, Savta," he said, pointing out the window. He sighed and pointed to himself: "*Ani po.*"

I figured that everyone else was at the store, and that Saba would rather be with them than home sick in bed. Just as I was thinking that he didn't look so sick, he began to cough. When he stopped, he leaned his head back on the pillow. I saw an empty cup on the nightstand.

"Tea?" I said, pointing to the cup.

"*Teh,*" he said, smiling.

I walked over, picked up the cup, and took it to the kitchen. I started boiling a pot of water, then searched in the cupboard for honey. My mother always spooned honey into my tea when I was sick. Aha! There it was.

Five minutes later I was back in Saba's room with a fresh cup of tea, the honey jar, and a teaspoon. Saba smiled as I set everything down on the nightstand.

"Honey," I said, pointing again to the jar.

"*Dvash*," he said.

I pointed at the jar, the cup, and my grandfather. Saba nodded. I dripped a spoonful of honey into the cup and stirred the spoon around. Saba took the cup from me and sipped slowly.

Ben appeared in the doorway, rubbing his eyes. I explained why our parents were gone and Saba was still in bed.

"Do you want breakfast?" I asked him.

"*Ess, ess*," Saba said, reminding me of the time Bubbe had tried to use that word, the Yiddish word for "eat," in one of our Scrabble games.

"Saba wants you to go eat," I said, using my bossiest voice.

"Fine," Ben mumbled, sulking away. He returned a few minutes later with a banana and a backgammon board.

"*Sheshbesh*!" Saba exclaimed, pointing to the board, and then sneezed twice. He shook his finger when Ben put the game on the bed.

"*Holeh*," he said, pointing at himself. "No, no." He shook his finger.

"What does that mean, Molly?"

"I think it means he's sick and doesn't want you to get too close."

"Oh. He can still play, though. Saba, backgammon?" Ben held the game up and climbed onto the bed. Saba began to protest.

"I don't think Mom is going to want you on Saba's bed when he's sick, Ben," I said quickly.

"Are you playing, or what?"

Three games and three cups of tea later, Ben declared himself backgammon king. He'd beaten me twice and Saba once. We all sat next to each other on the bed. Just as we were about to start up a fourth game, we heard a sound at the front door. Ben quickly scooped all the pieces of the game into the box. We jumped off the bed and ran across the room to sit in chairs. Saba smoothed down the sheets and pulled the covers up around his chest. As our mother entered the room, he said, "*Holeh, holeh*" and waved his hand as if shooing us away.

"Kids! What are you doing in here? Let's go; let your grandfather rest. Do you want to get sick too?"

Ben and I slipped out to the living room. A minute later, Mom joined us there.

"Okay, I'd better get started on lunch. Savta will be here in a few minutes to help me get it ready, and your father will be along soon." She slumped down on the couch. "That store is a lot of work." Her hair was coming loose from its ponytail, and several sweaty strands hung down around her face.

"Do you want us to come help?" I asked.

"No, no, it'll be fine . . . I think. Moshe is coming soon to help out. Thursdays are the worst, because everyone needs fish for Friday night and Saturday. Savta is very busy preparing chickens in the back room. Earlier in the week, business is a lot slower." She brushed the back of her hand across her forehead. "It is so hot in there."

"So Saba usually does all that work by himself?"

Mom stared ahead blankly. "I don't know how."

We heard someone come in the front door. Savta stuck her head in the doorway and spoke to my mother.

Mom groaned as she stood up from the couch. "I'm going to sleep well tonight."

As soon as Savta and Mom were busy in the kitchen, Ben and I slipped back into Saba's room. He was dressed, sitting on the edge of the bed wearing his typical short-sleeved white shirt and suspenders. I thought he looked better already.

"Saba, did you know I was on the baseball team?" Ben asked him.

Saba looked confused.

"Hold on . . . I'll be right back." Ben ran out and returned with a photo of himself in his uniform. He sat on the bed and showed the picture to Saba.

"Baseball. That's me, number twelve."

"Beis-bol?" Saba shook his head.

"Like this." Ben stood in a batter's stance, pretending to swing at an incoming ball. "Molly, make believe you're pitching."

I pretended to pitch the ball, and Ben swung again and then ran to three imaginary bases and home.

"A homerun! See, Saba, that's baseball."

Saba chuckled. "Beis-bol," he said, and nodded his head.

"Kids, what did I say?" We all turned to see Mom in the doorway, hands on her hips. She scowled at all of us, but the scowl faded when Ben said, "I was just showing Saba how to play baseball. I don't think he knows how."

"Yes, well, soccer and basketball are more popular here."

Saba spoke in Hebrew to their mother, and she answered.

"Saba said baseball looks like fun. He asked how many players are on the field. I said five, right?"

Ben rolled his eyes. "Nine players, Mom, nine."

"Okay, okay," she said, and turned to Saba to correct her mistake. Just then, Dad appeared in the doorway. We hadn't heard him come in. He looked exhausted. He wore an apron from the store, but both the apron and the rest of his clothes were covered with splotches of fish blood. He was a mess.

"Can I talk to you for a minute?" he said to my mother. His face was flushed.

They headed to the living room. Ben and I followed, lingering outside the doorway. Dad spoke in a whisper. At first Mom didn't say anything, but then we heard her say "Oh, no!" and, totally unexpectedly, she burst out laughing, so loudly that Savta and Saba came over to see what the fuss was about.

Mom was laughing so hard that tears rolled down her cheeks. Dad still looked worried. Mom started to speak in Hebrew, and I watched my grandparents' reactions. Saba smacked his forehead with his palm, his eyes opened wide. Saba and Savta looked at each other, and then they began to snicker.

The only adult not laughing was my father, who still looked mortified.

"Well, what happened?" Ben shouted.

"Yeah, tell us what happened," I repeated.

"Well, I'm glad they think it's so funny," he began slowly. "I never knew the store was such hard work. It takes me twenty minutes just to scoop the fish out of the tank. Then trying to hit it with that stick . . . At least five ended up on the floor, wriggling all over the place . . ." Even Dad began to smile a bit. "So, then your mother and grandmother leave me there alone, and I'm just about to lock up for lunch when a woman shows up and says she must get her fish right then for Shabbat. So for a change, it goes fairly smoothly, and I wrap up the fish and hand it to her. And she says that she wants to see the accounting book, to see how much she owes on credit. So I hand her the book . . ." Dad blushed again. "I didn't know that customers aren't supposed to see the book."

"Why?"

"Because," Mom continued, "Saba has a terrible memory for names, even people who have been coming to the store for years. So he puts little clues next to the names so he'll remember who is who." She giggled.

"My luck, that woman was 'the loud one.' She wasn't too happy about it." Dad sighed. "I should have looked first."

"We should have told you! It never occurred to us that someone would ask to see that book," Mom consoled him. Saba walked over and thumped him heartily on the back.

"*Ze beseder, ze beseder*," he said warmly.

"What did Saba say?" Ben asked.

"He said it's okay. I guess it's not the end of the world." Dad rubbed his forehead and chuckled. "What a day!"

Moshe showed up while we were eating lunch. The story was told again, Dad blushed again, and everyone laughed.

Saba insisted he was fine and didn't need so much pampering. In response, Mom produced the thermometer, which showed him to still have a fever. Saba reluctantly agreed to spend the rest of the day at home, and Savta, Moshe, Mom, and Dad returned to the store.

• • •

That afternoon, as Saba sat in bed reading a Romanian newspaper, I walked over to the shelf full of family photographs and picked up the one with young Saba and his siblings. Bringing it to Saba, I asked in my best accent, "*Aifo* Malka?" *Where is Malka?*

Saba took the photograph from my hands, sighing wistfully. He pointed to a girl in a simple white dress with a bow at the collar.

"Malkaleh," he said, and brushed the dust off the glass with his sleeve. "*Yalda tova*," he said softly, tapping the picture. Saba put his arm around me and smiled. "*Yalda tova*."

I remembered those words from Hebrew school. *Yalda tova*, a good girl. I leaned against his chest, feeling his suspender against my cheek. We looked at the photograph together.

* * *

When the other adults finally came home at four o'clock, my parents were exhausted. They went straight to bed and said they would sleep until supper. Meanwhile Savta went to work in the kitchen, where I heard pots clanging.

I walked into the kitchen and leaned on a

counter. Savta smiled at me and then turned back to her cooking. She had already begun preparing the elaborate meals she would serve Friday night and Saturday. Carrots, celery, and onions were set out on the counter, and pieces of skinned chicken were lying in a pot. Savta had just finished scrubbing the carrots. She chose a knife out of a drawer and began chopping them. I tapped Savta on the shoulder and then pointed to myself. Savta hesitated but then handed me the knife, pushing the vegetables my way. I began chopping, while Savta formed two loaves of gefilte fish, then mixed and flattened dough for cookies. Her energy amazed me.

Once I'd finished chopping and all the vegetables were cooking, Savta opened the refrigerator and took out half a watermelon. She placed it on the table along with salt, garlic, dill, and an empty jar. I sat down on a chair to watch, realizing the recipe for my delicious pickled watermelon was about to be revealed.

Savta chopped off a hunk of watermelon. She scooped out most of the pink watermelon flesh from the smaller piece and put it aside, leaving the green rind with only half an inch of melon. She carefully skinned the rind, removing the hard green outside. She cut the remaining rind into fat cubes and then stuffed them into the jar, along with many cloves of garlic and dill. Everything was stuffed tight against the glass. Savta stirred salt into a glass of water, poured that into the jar too, and sealed the top. I expected her to place the new jar alongside the other one in the refrigerator, but I was wrong. Savta beckoned me to follow, and I watched as she placed the jar in a sunny spot outside. I looked at my grandmother and smiled.

12

A few nights later, my parents and grandparents were watching television together in the living room my parents used as a bedroom. A newscaster spoke in Hebrew. Everything he said was subtitled in Arabic.

I sat down on the couch next to my mother. "Mom," I said.

"Hmm?" My mother turned to look at me.

"I was thinking that I might want to get a new bathing suit. You know, for the beach."

"Okay, sure. The one you have is getting old. Maybe we can go shopping downtown tomorrow."

"Great," I said, pleased. I did want a new suit. But I also wanted some time alone with my mom. Suggesting a shopping trip was the best way to get both.

The next day, Mom and I took the bus to the

center of town. We strolled down the main street and peered into the windows of bookstores, food stores, and clothing stores.

"The bathing suit store I want to take you to is down at the end of the block," Mom told me. "The mother of my best friend from high school still owns it."

"Really? What was your best friend's name?"

"Marta."

"Are you still friends with her?"

"Sure. She lives in Tel Aviv now with her family. I'm planning to see her next week when we're there. Maybe you'll meet her too."

"How do you stay friends when you never see each other?" I asked.

"We write. I see her every time I come here. You don't have to see someone all the time for her to be your friend. But I do miss Marta."

It seemed as if Mom missed a lot of people in Israel. I knew how expensive it was to travel from Israel to the United States, but I still couldn't imagine not seeing Jenny for years at a time. Not to mention my own parents and brother!

"This is the store," Mom said, pointing to a small shop with a colorful window.

We walked in, and the door jingled closed behind us. Someone shouted from the back room.

"That's her," Mom whispered. "She said she'd be right out."

A plump older woman emerged from the small room, which was piled high with boxes. She squinted at my mother, and then put on the glasses that hung around her neck.

"Luisa?" she exclaimed.

"Madame Fleishman, shalom!" They hugged for a long time, and then the woman stood back and looked at me, shaking her head back and forth in amazement. She and I exchanged greetings. Madame Fleishman and my mother continued talking animatedly. Mom pointed at me and the woman nodded several times, gesturing to the racks. She returned to the back room and began rummaging in boxes.

"Why do you call her Madame?" I asked.

"It's from back in Romania. Married women are called Madame. She says she has some new bathing suits that just came in."

Madame Fleishman came back with a pile of bathing suits in her arms. She ushered us into a dressing room, where I sifted through the pile. I tried on a flower print with a tiny bow in front.

"I don't think so," I said. "A little too heavy on the flowers."

Mom smiled. "I think you're right."

I exchanged the flowers for a polka-dotted bathing suit. The suit fit well. I stared at myself in the mirror. The hot sun had highlighted my brown hair with blond streaks, and my cheeks were a rosy pink. I turned to look at my profile. My body was changing.

"Do I look older?" I asked.

"Do you want to look older?" my mother said, laughing.

I shrugged, embarrassed.

"I'm sorry. You *are* older; I can hardly believe it. I can hardly believe that this year you'll become a bat mitzvah. It doesn't seem possible."

It didn't really seem possible to me either, so we were on the same page on that one. In the coming year I would stand in front of my synagogue congregation on a Saturday morning and help lead the service. The thought of it made me excited at the same time that it made me shudder. I knew it was a very special event, celebrating a child turning into an adult and taking part in the Jewish traditions as a member of the community. I liked that idea.

But everyone I knew looking at me as I sang and chanted in Hebrew? That was harder to wrap my head around.

"Did *you* have a bat mitzvah?" I asked my mother. I pulled on the blue bathing suit my mother handed me.

"No, I didn't. Bat mitzvahs were less common for girls in Israel then. But we celebrated in the family, at Savta and Saba's house. Dad and I will need to start planning your party as soon as we get back."

"Jenny's doing that too," I said, fingering the strap of the bathing suit. "She said she's inviting at least thirty kids," I added, trying to sound nonchalant. I looked at my mother's reflection in the mirror.

"You could do that too! You can invite anyone you want."

I smiled. Jenny and I had already spent countless sleepovers whispering about who we would ask, especially Jonathan, the cute boy in our science class.

"You *are* older," Mom repeated, sighing and smiling at the same time. She handed me a striped bathing suit with ruffles. "Savta and Saba keep saying how good it is to be with you."

I held the bathing suit in my hands and looked at my mother. "Mom," I said to the reflection in the mirror, "why didn't you bring us here before?"

"Oh, well, money mostly. The tickets are so expensive."

"And?"

"And? And, I don't know." She paused, staring down at the bathing suits in her lap. "Maybe it was because, if we all came here together, I didn't know if I would be able to leave again. Maybe I was afraid it would be too hard."

I looked at my mother. Irit and her photo album flashed through my mind. I wasn't the only one thinking about an alternate universe—that much was suddenly clear. The expression on my mother's face was so sad that I was tempted to change the subject, but at the same time, I wanted to ask the questions I'd been waiting so long to ask.

"Why did you decide to live in the United States and not here?"

My mother lifted her head to look at me. "Well, at first, your father needed to complete his degree. It was very important to him, and he was already halfway through when we met. Then we both got jobs, and we thought we would work for a while to save some money. Then we thought that maybe it would be easier to come to Israel from the United States rather than the other way around. It turned out not to be so easy, and after you and Ben were born, it just got harder. We never really decided; it just happened."

Madame Fleishman stuck her head around the curtain. "*Nu?*"

I knew that word. My mother said it to me all the time. *Nu*, how was the party? *Nu*, have you finished your homework?

Mom and I looked at each other. "I like this one," I said, pointing to the polka-dotted suit.

"I do too," my mother agreed.

Madame Fleishman pinched my cheek and plucked up the chosen suit, leaving me to dress.

"Molly," my mother said, then paused. "I'm glad it's not too late. I'm so glad we're here together."

"Me too," I said and smiled at her. Mom grabbed my hand and held it for a moment.

When we emerged from the dressing room, we found Madame Fleishman holding a box wrapped like a present. I watched the two of them argue for several minutes; Mom insisted we pay for the bathing suit, and Madame Fleishman pushed the package into my arms, saying no. Eventually, my mother gave in.

"How can she make a living if she gives bathing suits away to everyone she knows?" Mom said as we waved to Madame Fleishman from the street. Madame Fleishman waved back, shouting "*Lehitraot!*" Mom shouted the same as we walked down the street.

"What does that mean, lay-heet-ra-ote?"

"It means 'see you later.'"

"Oh. We're going to see her again?"

"Probably not, but you never know, do you? 'See you later' is so much better than 'good-bye.'"

We walked past a bakery. "That looks good," I said, pointing at the pastries in the window. A few moments later, we were standing at the bus stop biting into hot, puffy *borekas* filled with mashed potato. An old man waiting for the bus gave us a thumbs-up sign, and we beamed back at him.

I knew that I would write about this day in my journal later—though I had a feeling that even if I didn't, I would never forget it.

13

As our bus rounded the corner into the Tel Aviv central bus station, I spotted Meir waiting for us. I tugged my mother's sleeve and pointed at him, standing there with his hands on his hips and his sunglasses pushed up on top of his head.

"No matter when I see him, he always looks the same," Mom said, smiling.

"How long are we staying in Tel Aviv?" I asked.

"Just tonight, and then tomorrow we'll go to Jerusalem. On our way back we'll spend more time here."

When we stepped off the bus we were greeted by Meir and his fiancée, Ma'ayan. She wore baggy pants, an embroidered shirt, and black clogs on her feet. I was pretty sure she had the most interesting fashion sense of anyone I'd ever met. She shook hands with each of us as Meir introduced everyone, and then Meir ushered us to his car.

"I'm very hungry, are you?" he asked, and we all nodded emphatically. Our journey had taken four hours, and we'd eaten the fruit and cookies Savta packed for us about ten minutes into the trip. We were ready for dinner.

"Then let's go to Dizengoff," Meir announced. I didn't know what that meant, but it sounded like food, and food was good.

Dizengoff turned out to be a wide avenue lined with stores and restaurants. "The Fifth Avenue of Israel," Meir said, laughing. Most of the restaurants had tables set up on the sidewalk, where diners sat and surveyed the passersby—and the people walking by looked right back at them.

Meir and Mom chose a restaurant, and we sat down at one of the outdoor tables.

"Is everyone going to watch us eat?" Ben asked.

"Dizengoff is where you go to watch the people of Tel Aviv walk by, like going to the theater," Meir answered, putting his hand on Ben's shoulder. Then he spoke to the waiter.

"Meir ordered appetizers for us," Mom said.

"What kind?"

"Every kind. You'll see."

While we waited for our food, Meir and Ma'ayan answered questions about their wedding, which would happen in Jerusalem in less than two weeks.

"It'll be in the garden of Beit Ticho, the museum dedicated to the artist Anna Ticho," Meir explained. "There will be a lot of music and a lot of dancing."

"Yes, my friends have promised not to sit down the entire time," Ma'ayan said.

"Are you going on a honeymoon?" Ben asked.

"Yes, but not right away," said Meir. "Ma'ayan and her dance troupe are going to Europe next month for some performances, and I'll join her there."

"Do you often travel with your troupe, Ma'ayan?" Mom asked.

"We perform mostly in Israel but tour a bit abroad. It takes a lot of energy, but it's also a lot of fun."

"And you, Meir, what are you sculpting these days?"

Meir shrugged. "You'll see. You'll come to my studio after Jerusalem."

The waiter returned, carrying twenty small dishes on his tray. He set each of them down on the table, followed by baskets of warm pita. I gazed at all the plates of colorful food.

"Would you like me to tell you what everything is?" Ma'ayan asked. Ben and I nodded.

"Well," she said, pointing to the plates, "this is hummus, tahini, baba ghanoush . . . do you know what that is?"

I shook my head.

"Eggplant, very good eggplant, made like a dip. Let's see, green and black olives of course, and Israeli salad, Turkish salad, Moroccan cigars . . ."

"Like skinny egg rolls filled with meat," Dad said, and Ma'ayan laughed.

"Very delicious ones. There are pickles and stuffed grape leaves too. I hope you enjoy everything."

We tore off pieces of pita and dipped and scooped, tasting all the new foods. I listened closely to the adults' conversation. I was especially interested in finding out more about Ma'ayan. She told us her parents were immigrants from England and she'd grown up in Jerusalem.

"My parents always spoke English at home when they wanted to tell secrets. So I learned to understand."

"Mine do that in Hebrew!" I said. "But I have a long way to go before I'll understand."

Ma'ayan smiled at me. "I know how you feel.

But every word brings you closer to unlocking the secrets of a language. Anyway, there are ways to get even with your parents. My sister and I learned Arabic in school and we spoke that to each other whenever *we* had a secret!"

"Don't give them any ideas," Dad warned jokingly.

"Too late," she answered, winking at me.

Meir looked around the table. The small white plates were wiped clean. "Anyone want more to eat?"

We all shook our heads. "I'm stuffed," Ben said, speaking for all of us.

"Coffee? Hot chocolate for the kids?"

We agreed, and when the waiter brought the drinks, he also brought a platter of pastries. Meir chose several, ignoring protests from the adults.

"These are different Middle Eastern desserts, mostly made with phyllo dough, honey, and pistachio nuts. This is baklava, and this one is called a bird's nest in English." The pastry lived up to its name, with a phyllo dough nest and crushed pistachios in the middle. Somehow we managed to devour all of the treats, licking sticky fingers when everything was gone.

A man walked up to our table and slapped Meir on the back. Meir turned around and shook his hand. "Itai, this is my family from America. It's time for us to test your English."

Itai raised his eyebrows. "Good evening," he said slowly.

"Good enough. Sit." And Meir pulled a chair over to the table.

Itai turned out to be a violinist and one of Meir and Ma'ayan's friends. His English wasn't very good, but he tried to talk to Ben and me anyway. He asked us what we'd already seen and what we liked most. I liked the way his eyes crinkled when he laughed.

We stayed at the table for a long while afterward. Throughout the evening, whenever Meir, Ma'ayan, or Itai spotted someone they knew, they'd call out, and the person would join us to talk and drink a cup of coffee. Occasionally the conversation lapsed into full-time Hebrew and Ma'ayan would remind everyone to try to speak in English. When we all stood up to go home and go to sleep, we didn't say good-bye but "*Lehitraot*—see you at the wedding!"

14

Dear Bubbe,

Today the six of us squeezed into Meir's car and drove to Jerusalem. It's beautiful here! We walked around for hours, and Meir and Ma'ayan showed us so many things. I just asked Mom how to spell some words so I can try and write it all down.

This evening we stood on the Mount of Olives and looked out over the Old City of Jerusalem. The sun was setting, and the buildings glowed as if they really were made of gold. We looked out over the ancient stone walls and the two mosques, the Dome of the Rock, with its golden dome, and the mosque of Al-Aqsa, which has a silver one. Meir talked about what a holy city this is for Jews, Muslims, and Christians.

We walked to the Western Wall, and I could hardly believe I was looking at a wall that was part of the Temple built two thousand years ago. Dad, Meir, and Ben went over to the men's side. Mom, Ma'ayan, and I walked up to the Wall on the women's side. People prayed everywhere. I saw someone write on a piece of paper and slip it into a crack in the wall. Mom told me people write special prayers and messages and tuck them into the cracks because the Wall is such a holy place. I wanted to write a message, so she gave me some paper and a pen. I wrote something I've been thinking about ever since I got here, about my family, about all of us. I reached up as high as I could and squeezed the note into a crack. People prayed and sang all around me. It felt special in a way I can't really explain. I whispered my own prayer.

• • •

Next day:

This afternoon we walked through the Arab market, the souk, and I must have seen a million different things. Shopkeepers were selling rugs, scarves, painted clay pots, beaded clothing, and long embroidered robes. We walked up and down the narrow aisles of the market. Dad bought baklava and passed it around. I saw big brass pots and cases full of jewelry. Meir bought a beautiful purple flowered scarf and wrapped it around my shoulders, but Ma'ayan took it and tied it around my ponytail. She said I looked like a folk dancer. I'll show you when I get home.

***

The day after that:

This morning we had tea and borekas at a café on Ben Yehuda Street. Meir said it's another "people-watching" spot. The street is like a big outdoor mall, with no cars and lots of stores and restaurants. When I said that to Dad he laughed and said malls were just places like Ben Yehuda Street with a roof stuck on top.

After that we drove around to see the Knesset, the government building, and the Israel Museum. While we were there, we walked into a building shaped like a big white pot. That's where the Dead Sea Scrolls are kept, and the building is supposed to look like the covers of the pots they were found in. Meir explained that the scrolls are extremely old and had been hidden in caves near the Dead Sea for two thousand years. The Bible was written on the scrolls, and some parts are almost exactly the same as the version people still read today.

We saw the Chagall windows—beautiful stained glass windows that show the twelve tribes of Israel. I remembered the tribes from Hebrew school. Most of the day we just walked and looked around. Tonight we ate dinner in a Chinese restaurant!

Mom's calling me—I'll write more later . . .

A whole day later:

Have you ever covered yourself in mud and baked in the sun? We did that today at the Dead Sea, after we'd floated in it for a while. You seriously float and you don't sink. I bought a postcard of a man sitting up in the water reading a newspaper! Meir said it's impossible to swim or even go underwater in the Dead Sea because there's so much salt in it. That's why it's called Yam HaMelach, the Salt Sea. After we got out of the water, we went to the mud baths. Putting mud on your body is supposed to make you absolutely beautiful. Well, anyway, that's what Meir said to Mom, right before she threw some mud at him.

This morning we went to Masada, AT DAWN. I've never seen the sun rise before, but we saw it today from the top of a mountain. The name "Masada" means fortress, and Meir told us about the Jews in 70 C.E. who defended themselves from the Romans there. When the sun came up it made the whole mountain turn orange, like rust. I'm so glad I was there to see it.

Meir tapped his hand on the steering wheel. "We're early," he mumbled.

"For what?" Mom asked.

"For my surprise. Come on, let's walk down Dizengoff until it's time."

Even with our prodding and some pretty relentless tickling, Meir wouldn't tell us what he'd planned. We got out of his cramped car and stretched our legs.

"Isn't it amazing how you can leave the beautiful hills of Jerusalem and, in only one hour, arrive at the billboards of Tel Aviv?" Dad said. "I've always been struck by the balance of the ancient and the modern in Jerusalem, in this whole country."

Ma'ayan nodded. "I feel that way whenever I'm in Jerusalem. I look out at the ancient stones, and it puts things in perspective for me."

We strolled down Dizengoff Street, looking into store windows. Ma'ayan, Mom, and I lingered outside a fashion boutique, staring at the window display.

"Now that is a whole new perspective," Ma'ayan said, laughing. "Isn't it lovely?"

The mannequin in the window was dressed in a fluorescent orange mini dress. The dress had huge holes cut out of the material, as if a giant hole puncher had gotten loose in the factory.

"If you really like it, I'll buy it for you," Mom joked.

"Well, I do need a dress for the wedding," said Ma'ayan. "The white one seems so dull in comparison."

"Then again, someone might mistake you for Swiss cheese," Mom said, and Ma'ayan giggled.

My mother posed for a picture in front of the Swiss cheese dress. "I know I'll regret leaving it behind!"

I pretended to drag her away from the store as we all laughed.

"Okay, my dears," Meir called to us, "we're no longer early. Let's go!"

We followed him down a long street that led to the beach. I watched the sea peek up over the hill as we walked. The closer we got, the stronger the salty smell of the water became, and I breathed it in. My new bathing suit scratched a little underneath my clothes. Meir had already told us about the beach, so what was the surprise?

At the bottom of the hill, Meir led us to a small café close to the water. Sitting around one of the tables were Rivka, Yaacov, Assaf, and Irit, who all jumped up and greeted us. Rivka gave me a big hug.

"How was Jerusalem?" Rivka asked.

"It was beautiful," I said. "I loved it. I'm glad we'll be going back."

"I'm looking forward to it too."

"How long are you going to stay with us?"

"Just today, then we need to get back to work tomorrow. The kibbutz is only an hour away from here. We wanted to surprise all of you and spend some time together."

"I wish you were coming back to Nahariya with us," I said, frowning in spite of myself.

"Me too. But I'd probably steal your bed and leave you to sleep on the floor, and then maybe I wouldn't be so welcome anymore," Rivka said, grinning. I grinned back.

We set up our blanket and towels on the sand.

Rivka pulled lotions, water bottles, sunglasses, and an inflatable raft out of a small bag. Yaacov blew up the raft, one puff at a time. It was large enough for several people to sit on.

"Who wants to go for a swim?" he asked in two languages, and Assaf and Ben ran with him into the waves. I poured a few drops of suntan lotion on my very white stomach and rubbed it in.

"Put more on," Mom said. "We don't want you as red as a lobster when you leave. By the way, you look nice in your new bathing suit."

I smiled and leaned back on my towel. The sun was very hot, and I felt like my skin was already starting to sizzle. I closed my eyes and listened to the adults talking in Hebrew. I imagined Ma'ayan in the Swiss cheese dress, walking down the aisle. Then I imagined her in a long, white, flowing dress, with a pretty veil and roses in her bouquet. The picture in my mind became hazy, and everyone seemed to float around.

"Molly, Molly, get up. You've been lying there too long."

I opened my eyes and sat up. Beads of sweat dripped down my forehead. My head hurt.

"I think I fell asleep."

"I think so too," Mom said. "Why don't you go into the water? It'll wake you up."

I saw that Meir and Irit had joined Yaacov and the rest in the water. They were bobbing up and down in the waves, holding onto the raft. I stood up and wobbled a little, then walked down to the sea. I waded in, and the cool water soothed my skin. I was chin deep when I reached the raft, but I didn't have enough time to grab hold of it before a large wave came and washed over my head. Once it passed, I steadied myself and rubbed water out of my eyes, tasting the salt in my mouth.

"Don't drink the sea, Molly. There isn't enough of it for all of us," Meir teased.

"Hey, let's all get on the raft!" Ben shouted, and Meir translated. The kids scrambled on first, with Meir and Yaacov helping us. I sat on the edge with Irit and scooped up a big piece of seaweed floating on the water. Irit put it on her father's head, making a green wig. She and I laughed at him and he growled back, like any good sea monster would. Then he and Meir climbed onto the raft and we all floated together, splashing each other with water and throwing seaweed back and forth. We waved to the adults still on shore, but no one noticed us. Irit held a string of seaweed up to her neck like a necklace. Ben made a beard and mustache for himself, and everyone laughed.

Suddenly, a huge wave rolled over the raft, knocking us all off and into the water. I felt someone on top of me. I tried to push them off but couldn't. I opened my eyes to murky green water, and saw arms and legs flailing.

Terror shot through me. I couldn't breathe . . .

Suddenly the body on top of me moved and I felt someone grab my arm and yank me up to the surface. I came up coughing and couldn't catch my breath. Meir held me until the coughing stopped and I could breathe again.

"Are you okay?" he asked me gently.

I coughed again and nodded. "I should have listened to you and not tried drinking the sea."

Meir smiled and squeezed me close to him. "You scared me. When we came up we couldn't see you and Assaf. It seems you were tangled up underwater." I saw Assaf sitting on the raft, his face red from coughing.

"I think that's enough swimming for today. Let's go back," Yaacov said, carrying Irit and pulling Assaf and Ben on the raft. Meir carried me until we reached the shallow water, and then held my hand as we walked on the sand. Back at the blanket, Rivka wrapped us all in towels and rubbed our backs. With everyone around me and a warm towel on my shoulders, I finally stopped shaking.

A few minutes later Assaf tapped me on the shoulder. I looked over to see him pouring sand over my father's leg as he lay on his towel. Smothering a giggle, I got to work helping my cousin. We quickly covered my father's hand, and then his arm. Soon half his body was under sand.

"I can't tell you how wonderful this feels. Really, thank you so much," he said, but we continued burying him anyway.

"You have to say please ten times if you want Assaf and Molly to let you go," Ben said.

"No, that's too easy," Ma'ayan said, and spoke in Hebrew to Assaf. He smiled craftily and said something to Dad.

"What did he say?" I asked.

"He basically said freedom can be bought with ice cream sodas for you kids," Ma'ayan explained. "Otherwise, your dad's here for good."

Dad surrendered and we dug him out of the sand. We all walked back to the café, where we kids got ice cream sodas and the adults sipped iced coffees with scoops of ice cream floating on top. After the drinks were gone, Meir asked, "Does anyone want to see my studio?"

We all said yes, of course.

The studio was near the center of town. Meir unlocked the building's front door and we followed him down a long corridor with doors on either side. One door was open, and loud music blared from inside. Meir stuck his head in.

"Simon?" he called.

The man who appeared in the doorway was completely covered with specks of paint: his hands, his hair, his clothes, even his eyeglasses. He smiled at us and spoke with Meir for a few minutes before we continued down the hall to Meir's studio.

"I'm guessing he's a painter," Mom said.

"You guess right. He's a painter of very large paintings."

"What are they like?" Ben asked.

"Very detailed. The people and animals look almost real. Some paintings are based on things he remembers from when he was a child in Iraq. Some show aspects of Arab and Israeli culture in interesting ways."

"Is he always covered in paint?"

"Always."

We followed Meir into a large room with a high ceiling. Tools and pieces of metal were strewn all over the floor.

"Here it is, the famous studio where everything happens, or doesn't happen," he said.

He pointed to a sculpture of a fish. "This is something I finished a while ago." When I looked closer I saw that there was a man sleeping inside the fish's open mouth.

"It's my own version of the story of Jonah. I think I really just wanted to make a very big fish." Meir smiled at me.

"What's this?" my mother asked. "It's beautiful."

We gathered around a smooth bronze sculpture in the shape of a man holding a baby. Neither figure had any features or other details, but the way the man was bent over the baby in his arms made it seem like he was holding something very precious to him.

"Will that be you someday?" Mom asked.

"Actually," Meir said, "I was thinking of our father when I made it. I was practically a baby when he brought us here. I imagine him holding me that way on the ship coming over, with his hopes for the new life he wanted us to have and the kind of person I would become." Meir smiled. "But maybe you're right, maybe that will be me one day too."

I stared at the sculpture. Something about the man's posture really did remind me of Saba. Meir, I realized, saw him just the way I did. Meir had said it was the way Saba might have held him, but a different thought entered my mind. This was how Saba might have held *me*, if he could've, when I was a baby. He would have looked just that way. And knowing that, being so sure of that, made me feel almost like it had actually happened.

Later that night, when I should have been asleep, I hugged my pillow to my chest and smiled.

All the pieces to my puzzle fit now.

I loved my grandparents. My grandparents loved me. I had a huge family full of people with confusing names and quirky personalities. But they were my family, and I was theirs. They lived in a country that was fascinating and complicated, where I felt more comfortable with each passing day.

My mother had been right about some things and wrong about others. She was right about how hard it was going to be to leave Israel, way back when she'd decided not to bring us at all. As much as I'd spent the first part of our trip counting the days until we could go home, I was now counting the days I still had left, wishing I had more. I didn't let myself think about saying good-bye to Saba and Savta and Rivka. It felt too hard.

Which was exactly how my mother had been wrong.

Sometimes hard is good. Sometimes hard is better, much better, than nothing at all.

16

The next day, as I was drying dishes from lunch, my mother walked into the kitchen.

"Saba and Savta want to take you and Ben into town, just the four of you. Is that okay?"

"Sure," I answered. "What do they want to do?"

"I don't know, they won't tell me. But you'll tell me when you get back, won't you?" Mom asked, tickling under my arm.

"Yes, yes, I promise!" I said and swatted my mother with the towel.

That afternoon Saba, Savta, Ben, and I rode the bus downtown. Saba wore the black felt hat usually reserved for Shabbat, and Savta wore a pretty flowered dress and white shoes. Saba bought ice cream cones for me and Ben from a street vendor.

"Chocolate and vanilla," Ben said as he peeled off the wrapper. "Saba, *todah!*"

Saba smiled and patted Ben on the back. We walked down the long street, looking into the store windows we passed. Saba and Savta stopped at a toy store and beckoned us to follow them in. They greeted the store clerk, who knelt down and pulled a box out from under the counter. Saba handed the box to Ben.

"What is it?" Ben asked, shaking the box. Something rattled inside.

Saba lifted off the box top. Inside was a shiny wooden backgammon board, with small black and white playing pieces.

"Wow, this is great," Ben said. "*Sheshbesh!* *Todah*, Saba! *Todah*, Savta!"

"*Sheshbesh*," Saba echoed proudly and ruffled Ben's hair.

Our next stop was a jewelry store. Again, Saba and Savta spoke to a woman behind the counter. The woman went to the back of the store and returned with a small square box. Saba took it from her and gave it to me. I opened the top slowly and peered inside. Resting on some tissue paper was a round gold locket engraved with flowers and vines, and my initials in the center. Saba lifted the locket out of its box and placed it in the palm of my hand, closing my fingers over it.

"Bat mitzvah," he said, patting my hand.

I understood.

When my friends and family gathered in the synagogue to listen to me read and sing, my grandparents wouldn't be there. Mom would tell them all about it on the phone, and so would I. Somehow, in my own way, I'd keep talking to them, making them part of my life.

I hugged them both tightly.

17

Less than an hour until the wedding! Our cab driver took us through the streets of Jerusalem and dropped us off in front of a large stone house. We walked up stone stairs and through an archway to the front door. Suddenly the door opened and Meir ran out. He spoke to Mom and then ran past us.

"What happened?" Ben asked.

Mom smirked. "It seems Meir is a little more nervous than I thought. He forgot the ring in his hotel room!"

"I could have gone back and gotten it," Dad said.

"I offered to go, but he said he hid it," Mom said and laughed. "And it seems he hid it from himself!"

"Well, it's early, it doesn't matter. Let's take a look at the exhibit."

We wandered through the rooms of the museum,

looking at Anna Ticho's artwork—mostly charcoal drawings of the Jerusalem hills.

"Does she still live here?" Ben asked.

"No, Anna Ticho died in 1980. She and her husband lived here for over fifty years, though. She left this house to the people of Jerusalem, to become a museum." I thought about what Mom had said about Israel being a difficult place but also a special one. So many people from so many different backgrounds had planted roots here, one way or another. And now, it felt like I was one of those people—a part of me belonged here.

We finished our tour and walked outside to wait for the rest of the guests to arrive. Meir returned, his car squealing to a stop in front of the museum. Soon, Rivka and Yaacov drove up with Assaf and Irit, then gradually the other relatives I had met at Savta and Saba's house joined us.

"Where's Ma'ayan?" I asked my mother.

"She's inside. At many Jewish weddings the bride sits on a special chair, like a queen, and all the guests go and greet her. We'll go see her soon."

We mingled with the other guests, who were gathering in the large garden behind the museum. Tables were arranged for the dinner. Bunches of flowers stood in vases. Musicians set up their instruments in a corner. I spotted Itai, the violinist, tuning his instrument. Itai saw me too and waved with his bow. I waved back and felt myself blush.

"Molly, you look flushed. Are you feeling okay?" my mother asked.

"I'm fine," I answered, annoyed. By the time I looked back, Itai was gone. I hoped he'd say hello again later on.

Simon, surprisingly paint-free, came outside and ushered the crowd into the museum. We were directed to a room where Ma'ayan was seated in a large decorated chair. People hovered around her, kissing her and wishing her well. I could hardly see her through the crowd.

"Meir and Ma'ayan have a lot of friends," I remarked.

"It certainly looks that way," Dad agreed. "There must be two hundred people here."

I stood on my toes and tried to get a better look at Ma'ayan. I inched my way closer and closer until I was standing next to her. My mouth dropped open as I stared at her. She wore a long, white, silk dress embroidered from head to toe. Her wavy red hair had flowers braided into it.

"You look really beautiful," I whispered, and Ma'ayan hugged me.

Simon asked everyone to clear a path down the middle of the room. I stood with Mom, Ben, and Irit. We heard the sound of a violin, and everyone looked toward the door. Itai entered, playing as he walked down the aisle. Four people followed him, each carrying one of the poles attached to a rectangular piece of velvet cloth, the *chuppah*. I knew the wedding canopy was a special part of Jewish weddings. Meir and Ma'ayan would stand under it during the ceremony. The people carrying it stopped at the end of the aisle and stepped as far apart as they could, so that the cloth looked like a flat tent above them. The rabbi stepped forward and stood underneath the chuppah, waiting.

Everyone turned to see who would come next. Meir walked into the doorway, with Savta and Saba on either side of him. They slowly made their way down the aisle. My grandparents were beaming.

Once they reached the chuppah, Ma'ayan's parents led her from the chair to take Meir's hand. Meir and Ma'ayan stood together under the chuppah with the rabbi and their parents. The rabbi spoke and sang in Hebrew, and I guessed that he was reciting blessings. He reached down and picked up a silver cup, giving it first to Ma'ayan and then to Meir. Each took a sip.

"They drink wine from the same cup," Mom whispered. "It shows that whatever happens, from now on they'll go through life together."

Next, Meir took the gold wedding ring and placed it on Ma'ayan's right index finger.

"Why did he put it on that finger?" I whispered to my mother.

"There's an old custom that says that there's a vein in that finger that runs straight to the heart. She'll put it on her ring finger later."

Ma'ayan put a ring on Meir's finger. The rabbi spoke, reading the *ketubah*, the marriage certificate, and reciting more blessings. Meir and Ma'ayan sipped from the cup of wine again. Then the rabbi held up something wrapped in a handkerchief.

"What's in there?" Ben asked.

"It's a glass," Mom said. "They're going to break it. It has many meanings, but the one I like best says that the couple's love will last as long as it would take to put all the broken pieces back together."

The rabbi put the handkerchief down on the floor

near Meir's feet. Meir lifted his foot and stomped down hard, shattering the glass.

"*Mazal tov!*" everyone in the crowd shouted and clapped.

Meir leaned over and kissed Ma'ayan. They hugged each other and then turned and walked back down the aisle. "Mazal tov!" Dad shouted, and everyone around us echoed his good wishes. I made my way through the crowd to reach Meir and Ma'ayan. They both gave me huge hugs.

Some people were already singing, and I could hear the musicians tuning up their instruments. Simon motioned for everyone to go out to the garden.

Outside, the musicians began to play and, almost immediately, a group of people started dancing. The music stopped only long enough for Saba's brother Yehezkel to say the blessing over the challah. Everyone was quiet as they listened to his soft voice. Remembering Rivka's story about how Yehezkel first started talking, I smiled. He tore off pieces of bread for Ma'ayan and Meir, and then asked for the music to start again. When it did, Meir took Ma'ayan by the hand and spun her around. They danced together with the whole crowd clapping.

I sat down at a table with Saba and Savta to watch the dancing. A steady flow of new dishes came out of the kitchen. I took a taste of everything.

Dad joined us and spoke to my grandparents.

"What did they say?" I asked.

"They're just a little surprised; they didn't know it was going to be such a big party."

"Oh. Well, there's one thing missing."

"What?"

"I don't see any *avatea-ach hamutz*! Where's the pickled watermelon?"

Saba and Savta both laughed. Dad winked at me.

Hours passed, and the party continued. Some of the people from Ma'ayan's troupe taught folk dances to the guests. I visited with my relatives, knowing I would need to say good-bye to some of them when the party ended. I talked to Erez and his girlfriend, who had come from the army. Every now and then I caught a glimpse of Itai playing his violin.

I heard the music start again, and people began to join hands. It was time for the *hora*. First there was a small circle, but it quickly grew.

"Come on, Molly!" Dad shouted to me from the circle.

I looked over and spotted Itai joining into the

hora, right next to Rivka. He caught my eye and smiled, waving me over. I was about to shake my head no, but then I thought, *Maybe sometimes you need to just jump in. Take a chance. Dance the hora.*

So I got up and walked over to the circle, waiting until Itai and Rivka spun in front of me. They welcomed me in, Itai holding my left hand and Rivka grabbing the other. We spun around and around, until the circle was so big it seemed that everyone had joined the dancing. Someone broke off and led us, snakelike, all around the garden. When we formed a circle again, several friends put Meir and Ma'ayan on chairs and lifted them, chairs and all, up on their shoulders. Everyone clapped to the music, and Meir and Ma'ayan held onto opposite corners of a handkerchief, laughing and bobbing up and down.

I was out of breath and panting when the dancing stopped. Dusk had fallen, and strings of little lights glowed from the trees in the garden.

"So you like Israel, Mo-lee?" Itai asked me.

"Yes I do. I like it here very much."

"Good, good. One day, you come back." He smiled down at me and tousled my hair. Then someone from the band called to him and he was off, back to his violin.

I sat back down with Savta and Saba, who looked as tired as I felt. Irit was asleep on her mother's lap. Ben and Assaf threw a ball back and forth. I watched the stars come out like tiny diamonds in the Jerusalem sky and leaned my head against my grandfather's soft shoulder. My fingers played with the gold locket around my neck.

I couldn't remember a happier day.

• • •

Dear Bubbe,

In a little while, our plane will land in New York. I'm probably going to see you in a few hours, but I'm writing to you anyway.

Savta and Saba came with us to the airport and Rivka, Yaacov, Assaf, Irit, Meir, and Ma'ayan met us there. Savta looked very sad, so I held her hand. Rivka invited Ben and me to come back by ourselves whenever we want and stay with her on the kibbutz. Maybe I will. When it was time to go we all hugged and kissed, and then we asked some guy to take a picture of us, all together.

Dad says you'll be waiting for us at the airport. I can't wait to see you, Bubbe. I can't wait to tell you everything.

ABOUT THE AUTHOR

Esty Schachter has written two novels for middle-grade and young adult readers, *Anya's Echoes* and *Waiting for a Sign*. She lives in Ithaca, New York.